Fresh as a Daisy

The Diamond Bay Series

By
Rose Bak

FRESH AS A DAISY
© 2020 by Rose Bak

For all the faithful puppies.

About This Book

Opposites attract – or they repel.

Retired from the military, Red O'Brian is starting a new chapter in his life by opening a tattoo shop on the Oregon coast. He figures his small business will be a perfect fit for the quirky beach town of Diamond Bay. But there's one obstacle in his way – Daisy Hunnicutt.

The conservative Town Services Manager is sure that a tattoo shop will bring nothing but crime and trouble to the small town she loves. When Daisy denies Red's business permit, Red goes to battle – for his business and his heart.

Daisy has no interest in dating an alpha male, no matter how hot he is. She has worked hard to leave her past behind and become a strong, independent woman. There's a ten-foot wall – and a 180-pound dog – between them, but Red's not about to give up on the woman he loves. Can he convince her that their differences are just skin deep?

"Fresh as a Daisy" is the second book in the Diamond Bay series. Each book in the series is standalone featuring a mature couple, steamy scenes, and a guaranteed HEA.

Warning: This book contains references to past abuse.

Want a free book? Sign up for my newsletter[1] to be the first to know about new books and special sales. No spamming, I promise. Click here[2] to sign up for my newsletter and get your free book.

---

1.   https://storyoriginapp.com/giveaways/62ee758e-068f-11eb-904e-c373f6014fe1

2.   https://storyoriginapp.com/giveaways/62ee758e-068f-11eb-904e-c373f6014fe1

Red

We regret to inform you that your application for a business permit has been denied.

"What the hell?"

Red stared at the official-looking letter in his hand, then crushed the letter in his fist. His friend Mitch had told him that Diamond Bay was a town that was welcoming to small businesses and that the business permit process was just routine.

He had packed up his life to move here and open a tattoo shop of his own. Not once had it ever entered Red's mind that his permit wouldn't be approved. He had submitted all the appropriate paperwork and paid the fees. What was he supposed to do now?

He uncrumpled the letter and read the rest. It was from someone named Daisy Hunnicutt, Town Services Manager for Diamond Bay. Red glanced at the clock on the wall: 2:00 p.m. The town business offices would be open now, he would go see this Daisy Hunnicutt. There had to be some kind of mistake.

It was a short walk from his house to the town hall, less than a mile. Nothing was super far away in Diamond Bay. The beachfront town was nestled along the rocky Oregon cost, and separated into two main sections: the tourist area and the main residential area where the locals lived.

Town Hall was smack in the center of a six-block strip that included the fire department, sheriff's office, a medical complex and several other small businesses that catered to the locals. The elementary and high schools were a few blocks over.

"I'm here to see Daisy Hunnicutt in Town Services," he told the skinny rent-a-cop at the desk.

"Third floor."

Red spied the staircase and opted to skip the elevator. He was on the wrong side of 40 and after retiring from the Navy he had been working hard to keep in shape. He knew a lot of guys who were letting their bodies go to hell at his age and while he wasn't as cut as he was twenty years ago, he still took care of himself. Both his father and his grandfather had died in their 50s from heart disease and he was determined to break that cycle.

The Town Services office looked like every bureaucracy in the country. Older building. Worn out furniture. A scarred reception desk. Fluorescent lights. He smiled at the elderly woman sitting behind the counter. She had to be 75 if she was a day.

"Good afternoon Ma'am," he said politely, giving her a smile. "I would like to talk to Daisy Hunnicutt please if she's available."

After a quick phone conversation, the lady led him back to an office at the back of the building. He walked in, years in the military causing him to immediately assess the area out of habit. It was a typical office with a desk and computer on one side and a four-person conference table on the other. He glanced at the woman behind the desk as she stood up to greet him.

"Hi, I'm Daisy Hunnicutt, how can I help you?"

Her voice was soft and sweet, a direct contrast to the severity of her looks. Red estimated her to be in her early 40s. Tall and slim, her reddish blonde hair was pulled back in a tight bun and her face appeared to be completely free of make-up other than some shiny gloss on her lips. Large brown eyes dominated her face, carefully expressionless.

She was the kind of woman you might not notice at first glance but when you took a closer look you realized she was quite pretty. Red took a closer look and felt a stir in his cock.

Daisy walked around to shake his hand and he was struck by how conservative her clothes were. People in Oregon tended to dress super casual, yet she was wearing a long black skirt that reached her ankles, low-heeled shoes and a peach sweater set. An honest-to-god sweater set. He hadn't seen one of those in years. She looked like the middle-aged spinster librarian in an old movie.

She moved and he caught the faintest hint of curves below her unflattering clothing. He was always fond of a stern librarian fantasy. He wondered if she had glasses.

"Miss Hunnicutt, I'm John O'Brian, although I go by Red," he started, reaching for her hand.

She was tall for a woman, he estimated her height to be about 5'9", only a few inches shorter than his 6 feet. Her hands were long and slim but his larger completely engulfed hers as they shook. He felt a frisson of electricity run up his hand, as if he had touched a live wire. That was weird.

He met her eyes as they shook hands and had the strangest feeling that they were connected. He could feel his body urging him to get closer. He cleared his throat and stifled the urge.

"I'm here to talk about my business permit, if you have a few minutes?"

Daisy gestured him to the small table, then opened a file cabinet and pulled out a folder. Joining him at the table, she opened the folder and looked at the papers inside, her tone businesslike but definitely chilly.

"Ah yes, Mr. O'Brian, I have your application right here," she began.

"Red."

She looked up, her eyebrows raising towards her hairline. "Excuse me?"

"Please call me Red," he clarified. "Mr. O'Brian makes me feel like my father."

She saw a flash of humor in her eyes before she banked it. "Went with the obvious nickname, huh?" she asked, gesturing towards his red hair and beard.

Originally a bright red, his hair had actually started to lighten over the last few years. He was starting to see some streaks of grey. He knew in ten or fifteen years that grey would be white and he would look like middle-aged Kris Kringle in that old Christmas special "Santa Claus is Coming to Town." He didn't mind aging though, it beat the alternative.

He gave Daisy his most charming smile. "People started calling me that when I was in the military, and it just stuck."

This was the point in the conversation where people usually asked what branch of the military he served in or thanked him for his service, but Daisy just returned her attention to his paperwork without commenting.

"I see here that you applied for a permit to open a tattoo shop on the Promenade," she began.

"Yes. Diamond Bay is one of the only tourist towns on the coast that doesn't have its own tattoo shop," he informed her.

Her eyes flashed with irritation but again she quickly neutralized it. "That's a point of pride for us, in my book."

He was taken aback. "You don't like tattoo shops?" he asked.

"No Mr. O—uh, Red – I don't. Tattoo shops bring crime and vandalism and other unsavory activity, and I don't want that in my town." Her face was impassive, and her tone even, but that didn't fully hide the judgmental edge to her words.

"Did I move into the Footloose town?" he asked incredulously. "Tattoo shops are totally mainstream now, and they bring in good revenue for cities and towns."

Daisy shook her head but allowed him to continue.

"You have a liquor store and not one but two pot stores that have opened in Diamond Bay since recreational marijuana was legalized, and you're seriously worried about a tattoo shop? Are you kidding me?"

Daisy straightened her spine and glared at him. He tried not to notice that she looked hot with that fire in her eye.

"My job is to make sure that any business that comes to this town is a benefit to the town, its citizens, and its economy. Your tattoo shop....," her nose wrinkled in disgust, "will not be a benefit to the town."

Red felt himself getting angry and took a deep breath. He rarely got angry, he was a pretty even-tempered guy, but he didn't appreciate the bureaucrat's judgmental attitude. "If you'll just look at my business plan, you'll see...."

"Your application is denied Mr. O'Brian," she interrupted, closing the file folder with a snap.

"Did you read the business plan?" he persisted. "Or the revenue projections?"

"I'm not going to change my mind, sir." Her tone was as cold as the arctic. She shot up from her chair. "Goodbye."

"I want to talk with your supervisor," he replied. "Who is your boss?"

"My boss is the mayor, but if you want to protest my decision you'll need to file an official appeal," she said.

"OK then, I want to file an appeal. This is ridiculous. Who do I send the appeal to?" he asked. "The mayor?"

Daisy huffed in irritation.

"If you had read the letter I sent you, you would see the appeal process outlined," she pointed out. "As it clearly says, you should send me a letter telling me why you disagree with my decision and providing any additional documentation that you think is relevant for reconsideration."

"I appeal to you about your own decision?" he asked incredulously. "How is that fair?"

She sighed deeply like he was ruining her day. "If I don't reverse my decision after reviewing the additional information in your appeal, you are then entitled to petition the town council and present your case there," she informed him. "Again, the instructions are at the bottom of the letter you received. Now if you'll excuse me, I really need to get back to work."

Red stood up. "You'll be hearing from me soon then. I'm guessing that I'll see you at the town council after that. Goodbye."

Daisy

Daisy watched Red O'Brian stride out of her office and sighed deeply.

It wasn't like her to get flustered, but the entire encounter had unsettled her. As she returned to her desk her mind wandered to the man who had just left her office. He was about her age, she guessed. He had beautiful blue eyes, thick red hair and a neatly trimmed beard that didn't quite cover the smattering of freckles on his fair face.

Red was a couple of inches taller than her, about six feet she guessed, with wide shoulders, a trim waist and deliciously muscled arms. He had been dressed casually in jeans and plaid shirt, practically the Oregon male uniform, and beneath the rolled-up shirt sleeves she had seen what looked like full sleeves of tattoos on both of those beefy arms.

It's too bad he was exactly the kind of guy she would never date, because he was the first guy who she had been attracted to in a long time. Despite their unpleasant interaction she had been very aware of him the entire time he had been in her office. When he shook her hand she felt a flash of heat that had taken her aback. He had an earthy scent that lingered after he left.

She stifled another sigh as she opened her email. The town council would approve his appeal, she was sure of it. The truth was she didn't really have a good case for denying his permit. She was letting her personal feelings interfere with her job and she knew it. Yet she hadn't been able to force herself to do anything different.

Daisy had grown up upstairs from a tattoo shop and she knew more than most how dangerous they could be. Her father had been the leader of the infamous Seattle Devils motorcycle club when she was a kid, and probably still was. The tattoo shop he owned with his "old lady", also known as Daisy's mom, was a front for all manner of crime: drugs, prostitution, extortion, theft. Dear old dad's tattoo shop only catered to other MC members and the criminal element they ran around with. Everyone else in the neighborhood had the good sense to stay away.

To put it lightly, Daisy's childhood had not been an easy one. She had learned at a young age that she had to take care of herself. Her parents and their MC friends weren't worried about things like making sure Daisy got a good meal or went to school. She had practically raised herself, and looking back, she wasn't sure how she even knew how. The only examples she had seen of "normal life" were on TV.

No one in the club paid Daisy too much attention until she became a teenager. Once her curves had come in she started catching the attention of some of the other members, who thought nothing of flirting with a young teen despite the fact that they were all so much older than she was. At first she had been flattered by the attention, pathetically grateful for any perceived kindness after a lifetime of neglect. She spent more time around the shop, allowing them to practice tattoos on her, dressing in revealing clothing like the other women who hung around the club.

The attention soon turned aggressively sexual by the time she was fourteen. Women in the club were often shared between members and despite her young age the members had no compunction about using her body for their own gratification. Her father sometimes offered her up as a reward for MC members who pleased him. Her mother took her to the doctor to get her on birth control pills but was otherwise completely unconcerned about what was happening. It was the way of life in the club.

Her life had changed shortly after Daisy turned 16. A collaboration of local and federal law enforcement officers raided the club one rainy winter night. With the help of the intel of a MC member who was actually an undercover DEA officer, the cops took the whole club down. Her parents were charged with everything from drug sales to racketeering to trafficking minors, and she was whisked away to foster care.

Daisy knew her own statements to law enforcement had been used as evidence, although they had blessedly refrained from calling her to testify in court. Fortunately, the District Attorney's office had sufficient evidence without putting her through any more trauma.

The cop who had been undercover in the MC made sure that she was placed with foster parents who could actually help her. Her foster father Samuel Johnston was a cop who worked in the sex crimes unit and her foster mother Suzanne was an advocate at the local women's crisis line. Sam and Suzanne had a unique understanding of what Daisy had been through. They took her in and helped her heal. To this day Daisy considered them her family.

With their love and lots of therapy Daisy came to understand that she was a victim of neglect and sexual abuse. Looking back now, she knew that even though she had grown up fast, she had been much too young to consent or understand what was happening to her when she was a teen. She had always understood that saying 'no' would not be tolerated in the club.

Daisy thrived with her foster parents. She learned about nutrition and manners and living in mainstream world where people made their beds and paid their bills and didn't get into fistfights over dinner. She figured out how to dress in a way that didn't solicit attention, and to hide the various tattoos she had been given while living with the club.

She got caught up in school and went to college on a full scholarship. She studied government and public administration, which was about as far from her old life as she could get. She graduated college with honors, her foster parents sitting proudly in the audience.

After college Daisy stayed in Seattle and worked at city and county offices in various capacities for about 15 years before the job in Diamond Bay caught her attention.

She was recovering from a violent attack by a MC member who had just been paroled and wanted to share her "family's" displeasure that she had cooperated with authorities after the raid. The attack had been unexpected, and rocked Daisy's sense of stability in Seattle. The idea of making a new start in a small town near the ocean had seemed like the right thing to do.

That was three years ago and in that time she had grown to love Diamond Bay. The small town was friendly, but not overly engaged in each other's business like some places. Everyone was welcomed here, with no question and she had developed a small circle of good friends here. Diamond Bay was eclectic yet cohesive.

Although tourism was the primary industry in town, they weren't quite as overwhelmed with tourists like some of the other towns along the coast were. There were lots of activities town but if you got bored Portland was only an hour or so away.

Daisy really loved Diamond Bay. She would hate to see Red and his tattoo shop change her lovely little town. Logically she knew that not every tattoo shop was a hotbed of criminal activity, but she couldn't take a chance on being wrong.

Red's appeal letter came the next day. It was well written, promising significant benefit to the community, and disputing any relationship between tattoo shops and an increase in crime. Daisy just couldn't bring herself to approve it. It was probably inevitable that the shop would open, but she clung to the hope that Red would get discouraged and open his shop in some other town.

A few days later Daisy was in the weekly department head meeting. The mayor convened the directors of the town's bureaus – Town Services, Sheriff's Department, Fire & Rescue and Parks & Rec – every Friday to check in on town business.

As usual, Daisy was the first person to arrive. Her foster mother had drilled it into her that if you weren't ten minutes early you were late, so she made it a point to be a little bit early for anything she did.

The rest of the team trickled in, examining the paper agendas the mayor passed around the table. Try as they might, they couldn't convince the mayor to go paperless.

Mitch Erickson, the town sheriff, cleared his throat. "Before we get started, I would like to make a personal announcement if that's OK Madame Mayor."

Seeing the mayor's nod of assent, he continued. "I'd like to share that I asked Penny to marry me and she accepted," he announced proudly. "The wedding is next month, just a casual event, but I would like you all to come. You should be seeing your invitations any day now."

The table erupted with congratulations. Daisy was happy for Mitch. He seemed like a great guy, and she had worked with his fiancée Penny last fall when she had been hired to overhaul the town's website. Penny was awesome – strong, funny and super smart – and she and Daisy had socialized a couple of times with other women in the town. Daisy was glad that Penny and Mitch had worked through their challenges to find a happily ever after.

The mayor moved them to the agenda. "First up, planning for the monthly town council meeting." The mayor passed out another sheet of paper with the proposed town council agenda. Daisy shook her head, they really needed to convince the mayor to send things electronically. They killed a lot of trees in these meetings.

"One of the items on the new business agenda concerns you Daisy so we will need you to be available to testify at the meeting," the mayor reported. "Mr. John O'Brian is appealing your decision to deny his business license."

Mitch's head swung her direction. "You denied Red's license?" he asked in surprise. "Why?"

Daisy stiffened. "I'm concerned about the criminal element that accompanies these types of businesses," she said evenly, striving to keep any defensiveness out of her voice.

"Criminal element?" Mitch laughed. "Red was in the military police with me. We've been good friends for years. He won't attract criminals. If anything, he'll make the downtown area safer by keeping an eye out for criminal activity."

"No offense Mitch, but I can't make decisions based on who is personal friends with you," she replied, her tone turning icy.

Mitch's eyebrows raised at her tone even as she reminded herself that her decision was made based on her own personal biases. He was right to question her, and she would have done the same thing in his place.

"The town council is just going to overrule you Daisy," he said. "I've seen his business plan as well as the work he did at the shop in Portland. It's all solid. I wouldn't support it if I had any doubts about it."

She sniffed. "Well, then the Council can overrule it and take the responsibility when we're overrun by motorcycle gangs and thieves."

Daisy could feel him studying her, no doubt surprised by her strong reaction. She ignored him but felt a flush run across her cheeks.

"Well, it's in the council's hands now," the mayor said placatingly. "On to the next item."

Red

Red yawned as he walked into the gym and looked around. It was 5 a.m. After twenty years in the military he just couldn't seem to break the habit of waking up early, regardless of how late he went to bed.

The town council meeting was tonight. Red hadn't been surprised when Daisy denied his appeal, forcing him to request a review from the town council. Mitch had told him that the town council would overrule her decision, but he was still a bit anxious about it. What if he had picked up his life and moved to Diamond Bay for nothing?

He had been up late researching documentation and statistics to support his assertion that a tattoo shop would be beneficial for the town. Since Daisy Hunnicutt's reason for the denial seemed to be based solely on her prejudiced assumption that the shop would attract criminal activity, he wanted to be ready to prove her wrong.

Well, speak of the devil, he thought to himself.

Apparently Daisy Hunnicutt was an early riser too. She was running on the farthest of the six treadmills lined up along the wall in the tiny gym. Without thinking, he strode over to where she was working out.

Daisy was maintaining a steady pace, wearing headphones, gaze fixed on the TVs overhead. She was still covered from ankle to neck, but unlike her conservative outfit last week, this one showed off a banging body for a woman her age. She was wearing running tights that lovingly hugged her long, toned legs and slim hips, and a formfitting long-sleeved tech tee that revealed surprisingly large breasts for such a slim frame. Red felt his shorts tighten.

He stopped in front of her treadmill, staring at her until she looked down. She started, almost tripping, before she caught herself with a hand on the side bar. Removing the ear bud from one ear, she said, "Can I help you?" as if she had never seen him before.

Red didn't like to brag, but he knew he was memorable. Between his red hair and beard, and his buff upper body, women usually remembered him. But he'd play along.

"Hi Daisy, Red O'Brian, we met a couple of weeks ago," he reminded her politely.

She continued running, her face impassive. "Uh huh. Yes, I remember."

Great conversationalist, this woman. He noted that she didn't appear to be out of breath despite her steady pace on the treadmill.

"I almost didn't recognize you in casual clothes," he said, deliberately allowing his gaze to travel slowly down her body and back.

Her eyes flared with irritation and she hit the emergency stop on the treadmill. "Was there something you wanted Mr. O'Brian, or did you just stop by to sexually harass me?"

Red took a step back, holding his hands up. "Whoa. Sexually harass? I think you're the one with all the power in this relationship."

She sighed, then wiped her face off with her towel before taking a long drink from her water bottle. He stepped around and moved onto the treadmill next to her.

"What are you doing?" she asked.

"Running. Same as you," he said easily as he pressed the buttons and started the machine. He lengthened his stride as the treadmill sped up. "I just wanted to say hello first, you know, to be neighborly."

She watched him for a few minutes before gathering up her belongings with a huff and leaving without a word. Red knew it made him an asshole, but he stared at her ass in those tights until she turned the corner towards the locker rooms. It was a good ass, firm but curvy. No jiggle.

Red spent the rest of the day obsessing about Daisy. Those fiery eyes, the slim body she hid behind her shapeless clothes, that delicious ass. Something about her fascinated him. He was drawn to her and wanted to know more about her.

He arrived at the town council meeting a few minutes before it was scheduled to start and was pleased to see that Daisy was already there. She was sitting in the second row, pouring over papers.

"Planning your defense?" he asked as he slid into the seat next to her.

She looked up, her eyes widening with surprise as she noted his suit and tie. Yeah, he could dress like a grown up if need be. Daisy was dressed in another loose sweater, this one over a high-necked shell, paired with another ankle-length skirt. A light pink gloss on her lips was her only make-up. Like every time he had seen her, she had her hair pulled back into a tight bun.

His fingers itched with the desire to unpin her hair and run his fingers through it. She smelled delicious, something lightly floral. Lavender, he decided. His body tightened, no doubt remembering the treasures hidden under those unflattering clothes. What was it about this woman that fascinated him so much?

"Were you raised Amish or something?" he asked, touching her arm. Once again he felt that shock of electricity.

She jumped slightly, then looked up from her papers in surprise. "What? No, I'm not Amish. Why would you ask that?"

He smiled and noticed her pupils dilate in reaction. When he looked down he was close enough that he could see her pulse beating furiously in her throat. Oh, this was interesting. Maybe she was more affected by him than she let on.

"No reason."

She shook her head and pulled her arm away. They both turned their attention to the dais as the meeting started. After moving through the approval of the minutes and the public comments portion of the meeting, Red's application was the first item under new business. He and Daisy moved to the speaker's table as instructed.

"Ms. Hunnicutt," the mayor called. "You may go first."

"Thank you Madame Mayor, members of council," she started. "You have before you an appeal to my decision to deny a business permit to Mr. John O'Brian, seated to my left, to open Red's Tattoo Shop."

Daisy spent a few minutes explaining her belief that the shop would cause crime and highlighting that the crime rate in Diamond Bay was lower than surrounding communities. "Each of the towns I mentioned has a tattoo shop," she concluded. "Given the connection between these types of businesses and crime, I denied the permit."

Red ground his teeth but otherwise kept his expression impassive.

The council members shuffled through their papers. "Ms. Hunnicutt," one man said. "I've considered your arguments that this shop would attract criminals and find no basis for that assumption. How is it any different than the marijuana dispensary or the liquor store?"

"If I may, Councilman Smith, I have attached several references showing how tattoo shops in small towns have caused an increase in crime and in fact are often fronts for widespread organized criminal activity."

"Yes," the councilman interrupted, "But none of these cases are from any time in the last twenty years. Practically every town in America has a tattoo shop now, and everyone from college kids to my own grandmother frequents tattoo shops."

Another council person spoke up. "I believe that Mr. O'Brian's business plan is quite thorough, and his revenue projections are impressive," the woman said. "Mr. O'Brian is a veteran who served with the military police. Also, the Sheriff himself has submitted a letter vouching for him. If the sheriff isn't worried about increased crime, I don't know why you are Ms. Hunnicutt."

Daisy's head spun in Red's direction and her eyes narrowed briefly, shooting him a quick glare before she caught herself and schooled her features again. She looked stoically towards the dais again.

Councilman Smith spoke again. "I see no legitimate reason for your decision Ms. Hunnicutt. I would like to make a motion to approve the business permit for Red's Tattoo Shop."

"Seconded," a woman at the end called.

"All in favor?" the mayor asked.

"Aye". Five voices spoke in unison.

"The motion passes unanimously," the mayor announced. "The permit is approved. Next on the agenda please."

Daisy gathered her papers and moved quickly out of the room, her spine ramrod straight. Red followed her without conscious thought. He was thrilled about the council's decision, but he still felt a strong desire to make sure Daisy was OK. He had a feeling she wasn't often overruled.

She was heading back to her office on the other side of the building in such a snit she didn't hear him behind her. She turned around to close her office door then jumped when she saw him, one hand going to her chest.

"Jesus Christ, you scared me," she gasped. "Why are you following me? What do you want?"

"For one thing, you to be more aware of your surroundings Daisy," he answered. "I know this is a small town, but you can't be too careful. What if I was some crazy person following you back to your empty office?" He felt a surge of protectiveness towards her that he couldn't explain.

"Your sanity remains to be seen," she answered wryly. "It's been a long day Mr. O'Brian and I'd like to go home. Your permit was approved, so we have no other business."

He lounged against the wall in her office, watching her. He knew he should leave, but he couldn't bring himself to leave her office. She seemed upset and for some reason it bothered him. He wondered why she seemed to take his permit so personally.

"Do you get this upset every time a permit you deny is overruled?" he asked curiously.

"I wouldn't know, I've never denied a permit before."

He felt his eyes widen. "You're telling me I'm the only person you've denied before?"

"Yes."

He stalked into the room and heard her breath hitch. She didn't seem afraid of him. If he had to hazard a guess, he would say she was feeling the same cloud of intense attraction surrounding them as he did. He looked down and saw her nipples perking up beneath the shirt she wore underneath her cardigan. She was definitely not immune to their attraction.

"Why are you so against tattoo shops?" he asked her.

"I told you Mr. O'Brian, this is a quiet little town and I don't want you attracting criminals to ruin it."

He walked over to where she leaned against her desk, stopping about six inches away from her. The air seemed to vibrate between them.

"I won't attract criminals, sweetheart," he told her. "Tattoo shops aren't automatically dens of illegal activity like you seem to think. I feel like there's a personal reason for your bias."

Her eyes turned sharp. "It's not a bias if it's based on facts," she responded hotly.

He deliberately looked her up and down again, like he had done at the gym. "Let me guess," he started, still standing closer to her than was socially acceptable.

"You were raised in an uber conservative Christian house, where you were taught to dress modestly at all time. Your daddy the preacher told you that people with tattoos were devil worshippers. You were taught you should never desecrate your body with ink because that would make you a slut who was going to hell. Am I close?"

He was surprised when she started laughing hysterically. Her laugh was musical, and her smile lit up her face, increasing his attraction to her. She was stunning when she smiled. He didn't know what he had done to make her smile, but he wanted to do it again every day.

"You could not be farther from the truth," she gasped, still cracking up like it was the funniest things he had ever heard. Red smiled in bemusement as she continued to laugh, tears running down her cheeks as she bent over at the waist trying to catch her breath. *What was so funny?*

"Oh my god, that's the best thing I've heard all year," she said, as her laughter finally died down. She hiccupped twice between giggles. "I really needed a good laugh today. Thank you."

Red was confused. "Why was that so funny?" he asked.

"You want to know why that's funny?" she asked, still laughing.

He nodded. "I'd love to know."

She suddenly slipped off her shapeless cardigan and dropped it on the desk behind her. To his complete shock she had a series of tats on both arms, from her shoulders down to just a few inches above her wrists. And they weren't girlie butterfly tats either. They were serious ink: a complicated array of skulls , animals, roses with thorns, and various symbols. Gang symbols, if he wasn't mistaken. They looked pretty old, the ink faded by time.

"Holy shit," he breathed. He knew his eyes were bugging out of his head. He could not have been more shocked. She was hiding all that behind those frumpy conservative clothes?

She smiled in triumph, then slid her skirt up from her ankles to a few inches above the knee. He couldn't miss that she had several more tattoos running up her shapely legs. *Where else was she inked?*

He raised his eyes to her face and for a moment she looked sad, before her face turned back to its usual impassive mask.

"My so-called daddy was no preacher," she told him darkly. "Thanks to him I had more tattoos on my body before I was sixteen that most people get in a lifetime. And that's the least of the what I saw and experienced."

Her voice shook a little and she cleared her throat. "Trust me when I say I know the shady shit that happens at tattoo shops. I lived it."

She dropped her skirt, grabbed her sweater and purse and strode out of the office, leaving him staring speechlessly at the place where she had been standing.

What the hell had just happened?

Daisy

Normally Daisy wasn't much for drinking, but after the day she had had, she wanted a shot of whiskey. Or maybe a couple. The weird run-in with Red at the gym this morning, a long frustrating day at work, losing the appeal at the town council meeting, then her little tattoo show-and-tell with Red, it had all left her feeling unmoored.

She carefully analyzed her feelings, as she had learned to do in the many years of therapy she had gone to after she was rescued from her parents. She felt anxious, embarrassed, disappointed in herself, and maybe a little confused by her strong attraction to Red.

She had trained herself not to feel strong emotional swings, but it seemed like that's all that happened when she was around him. And spontaneously showing him her tattoos, the physical representation of the life she had escaped? She couldn't figure out what had gotten into her. She carefully avoided showing the tattoos, if for no other reason than to avoid questions.

Daisy didn't go to bars very often, but tonight she would indulge. Just a little. She never had more than two drinks. Ever. The truth was that Daisy loved the taste of alcohol, and she knew it would be easy to start loving it a little too much if she wasn't careful. That's why she didn't keep alcohol in the house. It was too tempting for someone who came from a family that drank alcohol like it was water.

Since the liquor store closed at 7:00, her only real option was to stop by Jake's Bar. The bar was on the far edge of the residential side of town, a few blocks away from the Town Hall. It was quiet, as she would have expected on a Wednesday night. There was a handful of locals spread out at the tables, and the music was turned down low in the background. She hopped up onto a seat at the bar as the owner, Jake, came over, a towel draped over one shoulder.

"Daisy!" he exclaimed with a friendly smile. "This is a nice surprise. We hardly ever see you in here."

She and Jake had some mutual friends, so they knew each other a little bit. They were about the same age, and she knew he was single, but there had never been any attraction between them. Not like her and Red.

"Hi Jake," she responded with a smile of her own. "It's nice to see you. How's business?"

"Pretty good," he answered, "Especially when pretty ladies join me at the bar."

She rolled her eyes at the compliment as someone slid onto the stool next to her. "I'll have a shot of Jameson, neat," she told Jake. "And a glass of ice water please."

"Ah, the whiskey of my Irish ancestors," someone drawled to her left. Daisy stifled a groan as she realized that it was Red who had joined her. What was it with this man sneaking up on her?

"I would have pegged you for a wine spritzer girl," Red added with a smirk.

She shot him a glare. "Haven't you learned enough about making assumptions for one night?" she asked grumpily. He tilted his head in silent acknowledgement.

"I'll have what she's having," he told Jake. The bartender brought their shots and Red raised his in her direction. "Cheers."

She met his eyes, then downed her shot in one gulp. Ignoring the surprised look on Red's stupidly handsome face, she slid the shot glass towards Jake. "I'll have another, please Jake."

"Sure thing Daisy," Jake replied easily.

Feeling the warm comfort of her first shot, Daisy sipped her second shot slowly, savoring it. She sat in companionable silence with Red, both of them staring into their drinks and lost in thought.

She finally broke the silence. "Did you follow me here?" she asked.

He nodded and turned to face her. "I did," he said slowly, as if choosing his words carefully. "I wanted to apologize. I feel like I goaded you into revealing something you maybe didn't want to."

She was surprised at his insight. She hadn't expected that.

"It's true, I don't normally share, um, what I shared, with you" she responded. "I never do, actually. But I have to take responsibility for my own actions, Red. If you goaded me, it's because I let you."

He started to speak, but she interrupted him. "I also owe you an apology, Red. I made the decision about your permit based on my own history and bias, not on the merits of the application. That wasn't professional of me."

She paused to take another small sip of her whiskey, closing her eyes briefly in appreciation. God she loved whiskey. "The council was right to overrule me. I'm very sorry for the inconvenience."

He looked surprised but nodded in acknowledgement of her apology. "Thank you for that. Maybe we can just start over," he suggested, putting out his hand. "Hi, I'm Red O'Brian. Pleased to meet you."

She laughed, the whiskey already loosening up some of the tension she felt. "Pleased to meet you, Red," she answered, going along. "I'm Daisy Hunnicutt."

"Can I buy you another drink Daisy?" he drawled.

She shook her head. "No thanks, two's my limit."

He didn't argue, which she appreciated. She hated when people tried to force alcohol on her. "In that case, can I walk you home? It's dark out there."

She hesitated for a moment before answering, "OK." She felt her eyes widen in surprise. She hadn't meant to say yes.

It was raining lightly when the exited the bar, a typical Oregon night. Daisy zipped up her waterproof jacket and fell into step next to Red. They walked slowly, chatting about nothing as they made their way to her little house overlooking the beach. It was small and a bit dated, but it was all hers and she loved it.

"Well, this is me," she said, pointing towards her porch.

Red followed her up the porch, waiting as she dug out her key from her purse.

"Thanks for walking me home," she said, looking up at him. He met her eyes and she suddenly felt nervous, as if she was an 18-year-old girl standing on the porch instead of a 40-year-old adult. Attraction simmered between them.

Red placed one large hand on her shoulder, turning her towards him slowly, giving her ample time to pull away. She looked up into his impossibly blue eyes and saw the question there. He must have seen the answer in her own eyes because he slowly he lowered his head towards her. She leaned in to meet him.

Their lips met and Daisy caught her breath. It felt incredible. It was like the touch of his lips was something she had been waiting for her whole life.

Red gently nipped at her lower lip and she opened for him. His tongue swept in, exploring, and she moaned against his lips, moving closer to him. Her own tongue slid along his. He tasted like whiskey and mint. His beard rubbed against her jaw as he moved his head to deepen the kiss. She had never kissed anyone with a beard before.

She wrapped her arms under his jacket and around his back, exploring the hard planes of his back muscles. She could feel his cock hardening against her stomach and felt an answering rush of wetness in her core.

Red kissed her with a sweetness and intensity that made her breathless. Although her childhood had taught her not to trust men, she had enjoyed several short-term relationships over the years, always with nice, unassuming, stable men who were as far from the animals in her father's motorcycle club as possible. Yet none of them had aroused and excited her as much as Red did, just with one kiss.

He pulled back slowly, his gaze regretful. "I'd better go before we do something we're not ready for," he said softly.

She felt her eyes widen with surprise. In her experience, men like Red took what they wanted when they were ready, and they were always ready. She had misjudged him once again. They seemed to keep doing that with each other.

"Can I take you out sometime and get to know you better?" he asked. "Maybe get some dinner?"

To her own surprise she nodded. He smiled happily and leaned forward to press a chaste kiss on her forehead. "OK. I'll call you in the next couple of days and we can figure out a time."

She nodded again. "Good night Red. Thanks for walking me home."

"Goodnight Daisy. I'll talk to you soon."

He waited until she unlocked her door and closed it behind her, then turned and walked away while she watched him from her living room window. She didn't know what was going on between them, but she was curious to see what happened next.

Red

"How are you adjusting to life in Diamond Bay?" Mitch asked as he spotted him on the weight bench for chest presses. The gym was empty at this time of the day and they basically had the place to themselves.

"I like it," he grunted as he pushed through his last set. He settled the bar back on the rack and sat up to look at his friend. "I appreciate you helping with my business permit, man."

Mitch shook his head as they moved towards the free weights to do some biceps curls. "All I did was send an email confirming that we had worked military police together and that in my experience any concerns about potential illegal activity related to your shop were unfounded."

Red nodded. "I still appreciate it."

"No problem. I don't know why Daisy was being such a hardass about it," Mitch responded. "I've never seen her like that. She's usually firmly on the side of bringing in as much business to Diamond Bay as possible."

Daisy. His lips were still zinging from that kiss last night. That reminded him...

"About Daisy. I was able to talk to her some after the meeting last night and it's clear that something, um, bad happened to her in relation to a tattoo shop. I think it was when she was a kid. She mentioned something about her dad and criminal activity."

Mitch looked upwards thoughtfully. "Well that would explain her reaction to your permit, like it was somehow personal to her."

"Yeah, she admitted as much to me," Red said. "And apologized, to her credit."

They took a break between sets, each taking a drink from their metal water bottles.

"Daisy's a good manager," Mitch replied after he swallowed. "She's honest and, as you saw, takes responsibility. She's pretty creative for a lifelong bureaucrat. I think you'll enjoy working with her now that this is over."

"There's more," Red admitted to Mitch. "I think there's something between us. I, uh, well, not to sound like a middle school girl, but I like her."

Mitch's head whipped over. "You two?" he laughed. "Talk about opposites attracting."

"Maybe not as opposite as you might think," Red told him, remembering the array of ink covering her body. "I'd love to know the story about whatever happened to her when she was younger. Do you think you could look it up for me?"

Mitch was shaking his head before Red even finished the request.

"Don't do it man," Mitch warned. "The records are probably sealed but even if they aren't, you need to hear it from her. Take it from me, it will go very badly if she finds out you were running checks on her, no matter how curious you are or what your intentions are. I almost lost Penny because of that exact thing."

Mitch continued, "If she trusts you, she'll tell you eventually."

Damn it. He knew Mitch was right, but he had a feeling that knowing what he was up against with Daisy would help him avoid fucking it up. He was drawn to her, in a way he had never experienced before. When they kissed last night, he had been overwhelmed with a sense of rightness. Red had known in that moment that Daisy was the woman who he had been waiting for his whole life.

He already knew that Daisy was prickly. He had a strong suspicion that whatever happened to her would make her even more cautious about dating a guy like him. Hopefully he would be able to get her to open up to him and tell him her story eventually.

Red knew he should play it cool and wait a few days, but he couldn't help but call Daisy later that day. He liked her and was too damned old to be playing games.

"Daisy Hunnicutt," she answered her desk phone, her voice cool and professional.

Red deepened his voice. "Yes, I would like to get a business permit for my animal testing lab."

She paused suspiciously. "Red? Is that you?"

He laughed. "Yeah, it's me. How are you today Daisy?"

He heard the smile in her voice, and it warmed him. "I'm doing OK, and you?"

"I'll be doing better if you agree to have dinner with me tomorrow night," he said, doing his best to sound flirty.

"Oooh," she answered, sounding disappointed. "I have plans tomorrow. Another night?"

Red felt a sense of relief that she agreed to go out with him. He had been afraid that she would change her mind. They exchanged cell phone numbers and agreed to meet at the Crab Shack on the Promenade at the end of the week.

They exchanged a few flirty texts over the next couple of days. Red looked forward to Friday with an anticipation he had rarely felt.

He got to the Crab Shack fifteen minutes early. Daisy had warned him that it tended to be crowded on Fridays so there would be a wait. Sure enough, when Red got to the restaurant there was a good-sized crowd waiting outside.

Daisy arrived a minute behind him, her eyes widening as she took in the line. "Wow, I've never seen it quite this crowded," she said as she accepted Red's friendly hug. "How long's the wait?"

"Looks like 45 minutes to an hour," he informed her. "Should we think about another option?"

Daisy looked at him thoughtfully. "I think I have a better idea, if you're flexible. I have something I need to take care of."

"Absolutely," he answered with a smile "I'm up for anything."

And that's how he ended up flat on his back on Daisy's living room floor.

Daisy

"Oh my god! Are you OK?"

Daisy looked down at Red, who was currently almost completely covered by her Great Dane, Vinnie. She could see the bottom of his legs, one arm and part of his head, but the rest of his body was trapped under 180 pounds of overprotective dog.

"What. Is. This. Thing?" Red gasped, his voice muffled, probably because the sheer size of her dog on his chest was preventing him from taking a deep breath.

"My dog."

"Can you get him off of me? Please?"

"Oh. Sorry. Of course. Vinnie. Come!" she called, making her voice deep and commanding. The giant dog obediently jumped up and shuffled over to Daisy, sitting at her feet expectantly but keeping his eyes on Red.

"Good boy, Vinnie," Daisy said in sweet voice as she rubbed his head. "You're such a good boy."

"is it safe to move?" Red interrupted. "Or is he going to try to kill me again?"

"Sit up slowly and stay sitting," Daisy instructed Red. "No sudden moves."

Red gingerly moved to a sitting position, looking a little shellshocked. Daisy stifled the urge to laugh at his expression. She moved closer to Red and patted him on the head like he was a dog.

"What the...?"

"Shh," Daisy shushed him, then patted him on the head again, looking at her dog. "Friend, Vinnie, friend! This is Red, he's a good boy."

The giant dog looked from Daisy to Red and, assured that Red was no threat, wandered off to lay on the couch as if nothing had happened.

Daisy reached down and offered her hand to him, ignoring the frisson of electricity that ran up her arm when she touched him. Red hopped up easily but kept his wary gaze on her dog.

"I'm so sorry," she said. "Vinnie is very protective of me. It's been a while since I had a man in the house, and I forgot that would probably make him nervous."

Red shook his head and smiled ruefully. "I guess I should be happy you've got someone to protect you," he said. "I've been to war and I don't think I've ever felt fear like I did when that giant bastard sent me flying and then jumped on top of me."

Daisy could feel her cheeks turning pink with embarrassment. "Are you OK? Did he hurt you?"

"Just my manly pride."

She laughed. "Well, you did kind of squeal a little there as you hit the floor."

"That's because Vinnie landed on the family jewels," he explained.

She felt her face turn even redder and reached in her pocket for her cell phone. "I'll call in our pizza order, then we can take him for a walk and pick up our food on the way back."

"He's not going to attack someone on our walk, is he?" Red asked.

"Of course not," Daisy answered as if he was crazy. "He only freaks out if men he doesn't know get too close to me or come into the house and I don't prepare him first."

When Daisy had suggested that they skip the line at the Crab Shack and instead take the dog for a walk and grab a pizza, she hadn't thought about Vinnie's reaction. It had been a long time since she had brought a man home, and it was only natural that Vinnie would see Red as a threat, especially since he was a big guy with tattoos.

"Did you purposely train him to be a man-hating attack dog?" he asked curiously.

"Oh no, he started acting this way after the time he saved my life," she said. Her eyes widened and she slapped a hand over her own mouth.

What was it about Red that she kept letting personal information slip out around him? She was usually very close-lipped, even with good friends.

"I'll need to hear that story," Red said curiously.

"Let's take our walk first, Vinnie is eager to go outside after being alone all day," Daisy demurred, hoping he would forget about it.

Red pointed to where the giant dog was sound asleep on the couch. "Yeah, I can see that."

Daisy whistled and the big dog jumped off the couch, immediately awake and by her side. "Let's take a walk baby," she cooed as she put his leash on. "Then we'll get pizza."

They got back to Daisy's house a little over an hour later. They had been mostly quiet on their walk, each lost in thought. Red had seemed surprised that Vinnie was so well-behaved on their walk. Vinnie had been like that since he was a pup, totally attuned to Daisy's every command. He never tried to pull away from her, even when a cat went streaking by them.

After a quick stop at the pizza place they returned to her house with a large pie. Daisy gestured to the dining room table.

"Have a seat, I'll get plates and napkins," she said. "What can I get you to drink?"

"How about a beer?" Red asked.

"I'm sorry, I usually don't keep any alcohol in the house. I've got water, soda, lemonade or kombucha."

Red scrunched his nose. "Kombucha? Yuck. I'll take a soda if it's not diet."

She returned with two Cokes. Sitting across from Red, she slid a slice of pizza onto a plate. "Mmm," she said happily. "It smells delicious."

Red helped himself to a couple of slices of pizza, then pinned her with a serious look. "Tell me about Vinnie saving your life," he ordered.

Daisy flinched, but quickly schooled her expression again.

Hearing his name, Vinnie came trotting into the dining room, plopped down near the table and stared longingly at the pizza. A long stream of drool hung from his mouth. "No begging Vinnie," Daisy chided. "You know I'll give you the leftovers later."

Vinnie sighed deeply and wandered off to lay down again.

"Do you have any pets?" Daisy asked, hoping to distract him.

"Tell me the Vinnie saving your life story," Red redirected.

"Oh it's nothing," she said with forced casualness. "It was a long time ago and I don't really like to talk about it."

"How about the Cliff Notes version?" he suggested. "You got my curiosity up."

Clearly this guy couldn't take a hint, which was her own fault for letting the information slip in the first place. Red stared at her expectantly. She sighed.

"When Vinnie was a puppy, someone broke into my house and attacked me," she began in a carefully even tone, "Vinnie bit him and the guy went after him instead, which gave me enough time to neutralize the guy."

"Was it a stranger?" Red asked, a muscle ticking in his jaw.

"No," she said softly. Daisy willed herself not to think about that night, but the words unlocked the memories.

Coming home. Being thrown to the floor. Looking up into the face of the guy who was attacking her and realizing it was one of her father's "lieutenants" on a mission to kill her. The look of fury on his face as Vinnie attacked him with every ounce of his puppy strength. Grabbing a frying pan and hitting the guy on the head, knocking him unconscious just after he sent Vinnie flying. The panic she felt when she saw Vinnie hit the wall and not get up. The police interview. The animal hospital. The trial.

Thankfully Vinnie had recovered from the attack, and so had she. Then they had started their new life in Diamond Bay, with Vinnie her vigilant guardian.

She took a deep breath and willed the memories away. Willed herself not to cry. She had cried enough over the things that had happened to her. She was strong. She was a survivor.

Red watched her carefully. She wasn't sure what he saw in her face, but he backed off, changing the subject.

"We had a cat when I was a kid," he told her, answering her earlier question. "My mom never wanted us to have a dog. They made her nervous."

She breathed a sigh of relief.

They finished off the pizza, keeping the conversation light and avoiding any more probing questions. She really enjoyed talking to him and found that they had a lot of common interests. They both liked to read mysteries, and shared a love for skiing, running, country music and Star Trek the Next Generation.

Red got up to leave around 10:00. She walked him to the door, and he leaned in with a cocky smile.

"If I kiss you, will Vinnie tear my face off?" he asked.

She laughed. "No, now that you slipped him that slice of pizza he'll be your friend forever.

"I'd rather be your friend forever."

Before she could respond he moved closer. He gently put his hands on either side of her face and kissed her. His lips were softer than she would think they would be, and his beard tickled against her jaw. She could smell the pizza sauce on his breath.

Red nipped at her lower lip and she opened for him. Their kiss turned electric as his tongue swept in to explore her mouth. Just like the first time he kissed her, the entire world seemed to narrow to the two of them. It was spontaneous combustion.

Somehow he turned her until she was backed up between him and the door. He pressed close, turning his head to deepen the kiss even more. She met him eagerly.

Her hands snuck around to his waist and she pulled him even closer, grinding her pelvis against him through the fabric of her long skirt. He groaned against her mouth, his hands slipping down to her shoulders and pushing her sweater off.

He broke the kiss long enough to pull her tank top over her head, then he dropped down to kiss her again. It was dark in the hallway and she felt a sense of relief that he wouldn't be able to see her tattoos clearly. She moved her hands down, sliding beneath the waistband of his jeans to cup his butt cheeks over the fabric of his briefs.

Red started kissing down her throat while reaching behind her to unfasten her bra. He moved back a couple of inches as he released her heavy breasts from their confinement.

"Oh my god, you're beautiful," he breathed as he stared at her breasts in the dim light. Her nipples hardened under his gaze. He leaned down to lick around one nipple, then the other, before returning his attention to her mouth.

She felt him pinch her nipple and she moaned loudly, breaking off their kiss. "Oh my god, Red," she gasped. He dropped his head and left a trail of small bites down her neck and the top of her shoulder while still rolling her nipples between his fingers.

Daisy was grinding against his penis, hard and impossibly large against the fly of his jeans, trying to get herself off. They were dry humping like a couple of teenagers, she realized.

Finally, he broke off the kiss. "I'd better go before we get carried away," he said quietly.

He dropped a quick kiss on her forehead and left, promising he would be in touch. She stood there in shock, still naked from the waist up.

What the hell had just happened? She wondered. She had been so far gone, ready to have sex right there against the door, when he put on the brakes. She couldn't figure out why she was acting so out of character with him. A couple of days ago she would have said she disliked him, but now...now she wasn't so sure. She definitely felt like they could be friends – or maybe something more.

She was taken aback by him not pushing to do more, especially since they had such an obvious attraction. She had certainly felt the extent of that attraction grinding against her pussy. Apparently Red planned to take things slowly. As she calmed down she decided that was fine with her.

Daisy needed some time to process what was happening between them. She was conflicted about dating him, given his career. He seemed like a great guy, but she couldn't get past their obvious differences.

It's not his career that's scaring you, the little voice in her head told her. *He's blowing past all your defenses. He's getting too close. He will hurt you eventually, they all do.*

The voice in her head was right. She had never had a man affect her like this and it was scaring the hell out of her. She was already telling him her secrets and thinking about him all the time like a middle school girl with a crush. It was too much, too fast.

That night the nightmares came for the first time in almost a year. *She was being held down, turning blue. Vinnie was whimpering in pain. She grabbed the frying pan, heard the sickening crash of metal on bone. Suddenly her parents appeared, their eyes glowing with malice. They were after her.*

She woke up shaking, drenched in sweat, tears streaming down her face. Vinnie was standing next to the bed, his giant head on her legs, trying to comfort her. She rubbed him between his ears the way he liked and told her herself she needed to keep her distance from Red. Her subconscious was sending her a message.

She had learned a long time ago that people when people got too close they would hurt her. She needed to keep her secrets. She needed to stick with the only person she could truly trust – herself. It was the only way to be sure she stayed safe.

Red

"I heard you were on a date with Daisy last night."

Red put down his weight and stared at his friend. "How did you know that?" he asked curiously.

Mitch grunted as he lifted the weight to his chest. "Small towns, man. Nothing's a secret and everyone is a gossip."

Red lifted his eyebrow. "Even you?"

Mitch dropped the weight bar to the ground with a thump. "I'm the sheriff, I need to know what's going on to protect the community."

Red laughed. "Yeah, you tell yourself that." He paused, looking at his friend, debating.

"What's on your mind, man?" Mitch asked.

"I met Daisy's dog last night," he started.

"Vinnie? He's such a cool dog."

Red looked over at his friend. "Not when he was pinning me to the ground at Daisy's house."

Mitch fumbled his water bottle, spilling some on his chest as he barked out a laugh. "I had no idea that dog was such a cock blocker."

"When I asked why he was like that Daisy let it slip that Vinnie is overprotective because he saved her from an attack a few years ago," Red continued. "I got a little of the story out of her but didn't press her because it was obviously freaking her out to talk about it. Then when I went home I googled her and read the news stories."

Mitch groaned. "We discussed this. You know she's gonna be pissed when she finds out. And she will."

Red shook his head. "I'm glad I did. According to the news reports, the guy she was attacked by was some higher up in a Seattle motorcycle gang. It sounded pretty bad."

"Shit."

"He came for her the day he got paroled from prison," Red informed him. "Sounds like revenge to me. Daisy downplayed it but both she and

Vinnie were hospitalized after for their injuries. She moved to Diamond Bay a couple of months later."

"You think she might be in danger still?" Mitch asked. "Nothing has happened to her since she moved here, at least not that I know about."

"I don't know," Red admitted. "But I have a bad feeling about this. We should probably keep an eye out for her, just in case."

Mitch nodded. "Damn it, now I am going to need to look her up." He stopped and pointed at Red. "I can't share any information with you though, you're going to need to get information out of her the old-fashioned way."

Red nodded. "I just want to make sure she's safe."

"Stay close then man," Mitch said with a smirk. "I'm thinking that won't be a hardship for you."

"Ha ha. Let's do another set."

Red was working on setting up his shop a few hours later when he glanced out the window and saw Daisy walking on the other side of the street. She had been on his mind all day and he wondered for a moment if he was imagining her.

He raced to the door. "Daisy!" he called.

She looked up and waved but kept on walking. He called her name again and gestured for her to come over. It was faster than looking for the key so he could lock up and chase her.

"You bellowed?" she asked wryly as she stopped in front of him. As usual, she was covered from ankle to wrist in one of her spinster librarian outfits. He was starting to find it hot. He had it bad for her.

"I saw you walking by and just wanted to say hello," he said, dropping a chaste kiss on her cheek. "Whatcha doing?"

"Coming back from a lunch meeting at Pancake Hut," she said, refusing to meet his gaze. She seemed different from last night. Back to the cold formal Daisy he had first met in her office. "Well, nice to see you."

She moved to keep walking and he grabbed her arm. He saw a flash of alarm in her eyes and let her go. "Do you want to come in for a few minutes and talk, see the shop?" he asked.

She shot a horrified look at the shop behind him. "Oh god no," she said.

He tried not to be offended.

"I've got to go to another meeting," she told him. She practically ran away from him, calling over her shoulder, "Bye. See you around."

Red stewed on her behavior for a few hours. He was good at reading people and clearly something had changed. He suspected she was freaked out about their evening together. What had set her off? Sharing the story about her attack, or them making out afterwards?

He knew she was attracted to him, that was obvious from the way she had practically climbed him like a tree when they had been kissing last night. It had been all he could do to pull back from her. His body had been begging him to rip that long skirt off her and sink into her heat. Her body had sent a similar message. But things were happening fast, and he knew instinctively that her mind needed some time to catch up.

He also knew that she had been freaked out about him questioning her about her dog. Daisy clearly hadn't meant to share that information about the source of Vinny's protectiveness. It had broken his heart when she had stammered out the story of her attack over dinner. He saw the terror and pain in her face, as much as she tried to hide it. She had stared into space for a full two minutes afterwards.

He knew from his own experience in the military that she had been having a flashback to the event, and he had hastened to change the subject. The news stories he had read filled in some of the blanks, but he was intensely curious about the rest of the story.

After she had calmed down things seemed fine. They'd talked easily for the rest of the night, and then there was that hot make-out session against her door. Everything had seemed fine when he left last. She had seemed happy when he promised to call her. What had changed?

He knew she was still at work, but he texted her anyway.

Red: *Hey, nice to see you today. You free for dinner?*

Her response came back quickly.

Daisy: *No, sorry.*

Red: *Are you OK? You seemed a little distant earlier*

He waited a few minutes, obsessively staring at the little bubble that indicated that she was typing, then stopping. Finally, her reply came through.

Daisy: *I can't see you anymore. It's been fun hanging out, but I'm not really interested in dating right now. I'm sorry.*

Crap. He knew it. She was freaked out about what happened last night. He just wasn't sure what part she was freaked out about.

Red: *We can just be friends for a while*

Daisy: *Friends don't stick their tongues down each other's throats.*

Daisy: *You're a great guy, I'm sure you'll find someone soon. Lots of single women in Diamond Bay.*

Red: *Can we talk about this? Please*

Daisy: *I'm sorry. I'm just not interested. See you around.*

Red tossed his phone on the counter in frustration, unsure of his next move.

Daisy

"It's time for the bride and groom to have their first dance."

Daisy joined the crowd that was clapping as Mitch and Penny moved to the dance floor. Mitch looked handsome in his black tuxedo and Penny glowed in her vintage lace dress. She sighed. Her friends looked so happy. She was glad for them, really she was, but she felt a little sad that she would never have what they had.

What would it be like to completely trust someone enough to marry them? She bit her lower lip and willed herself not to cry. It wasn't like her to wish for things she couldn't have.

"That's a deep sigh, Daisy."

She turned at the sound of Red's deep voice. She hadn't heard him come up. The guy really was quiet on his feet. He was dressed in a dark blue suit and a white shirt, open at the neck. His dark red hair was slicked back, and his beard was freshly trimmed. He looked incredibly sexy.

"Hi Red," she said, trying to ignore the excitement she felt seeing him again. She had been avoiding him like the plague the last couple of weeks, but she knew they were bound to run into each other at the wedding.

She couldn't stop thinking about him and had second guessed her decision not to see him anymore about a million times. She hated to admit that she had dressed with him in mind, wanting to see if there still was an attraction between them.

"You look good," he told her, as if he had read her thoughts.

She was wearing a hunter green dress that highlighted her pale skin and reddish blonde hair. It was modest, as all her clothes were, but form-fitting. The dark fabric lovingly hugging her curves before flaring out to just past her knees. She had paired the dress with knee-high black boots. Her hair was pulled up into a French twist and she had applied subtle make-up.

"How have you been?" he asked, his face cautious.

She knew that he was hurt by her ending their budding friendship. He had texted her a couple of times since she told him she couldn't see him anymore, but she hadn't responded.

"Pretty good, Red, how about you?" she kept her tone distant but friendly.

They stood there staring at each other, not speaking. She licked her lips nervously.

"We invite you to join the happy couple on the dance floor," the DJ announced.

Red grabbed her hand. "Let's dance," he said firmly.

It was a command, not a question, and she should have been irked, but she followed him onto the floor anyway. He swept her into his arms, pulling her arms up to his shoulders and wrapping his own around her waist so she had no choice but to move close to him.

They swayed to the music, staring at each other wordlessly and communicating with their eyes. Red seemed to make a decision and pulled her closer so that they were pressed against each other from shoulder to pelvis. Daisy sighed and dropped her head to his shoulder. It felt oddly comforting.

They continued to sway together through the next song and Daisy could feel arousal building between them. Her breath was coming in short bursts. She could feel her panties dampening, and she was pretty sure Red could feel her hard nipples poking him in the chest through their clothing. And speaking of poking...clearly Red was just as affected as she was. There was distinct evidence of that against her lower stomach.

She sighed and rubbed her pelvis against his.

"You keep that up and I'm not going to be able to walk out of here without embarrassing myself," Red whispered gruffly in her ear.

Daisy pulled back slightly and lifted her head to meet his gaze. "I'm sorry I've been ignoring your texts," she said softly.

He nodded. "What happened? I thought things were good." She could see the vulnerability in his eyes.

"I got freaked out," she admitted. "I, um, don't trust people very easily."

He gave her a wry smile. "Really? I hadn't picked up on that."

She smiled back. "It's possible I overreacted."

He nodded slowly. "I've missed talking to you."

"Me too." She saw his eyes light up at her admission.

"Do you want to get out of here?" he asked.

She didn't think twice. She nodded decisively. "Take me home."

After a quick goodbye to the happy couple, Daisy and Red hurried out of the event space. "Did you walk or drive?" he asked Daisy.

"I drove. These boots are cute, but not comfortable for too much walking."

"They're hot as hell though," he growled, looking down at her long legs encased in black leather. "I walked, so let's take your car."

They were quiet on the five-minute drive to Daisy's house. They practically ran up the driveway and Red crowded behind her as Daisy opened the front door. Vinnie came bounding over to greet them, skidding to a halt when he saw Red. He gave a low growl. Daisy reached up and patted Red's head like she had that day when Vinnie had flattened him. "Friend Vinnie, friend," she said in a calm voice.

Red held out his hand, and Vinnie gave it an inquisitive sniff, then shoved his head underneath.

"He wants you to pet him," Daisy told him.

Red patted his head gingerly. "Good boy Vinnie, try not to eat me."

Daisy laughed. "I just need to let him outside for a few minutes," she told him. "I'll be right back."

She returned a few minutes later carrying two bottles of water, Vinnie trailing behind her. Red had taken off his suit jacket and was sitting on her couch, one ankle crossed over his knee. He looked good there. He patted the cushion next to him with a smile.

Daisy felt nervous. They both knew what was going to happen tonight, they had known it when she asked him to take her home. It had been a while since she'd been with a man.

She had moved through a series of short-term relationships over the years, but no one had ever affected her like Red did. When she saw him at the wedding, she had been filled with such a sense of yearning, such a sense of rightness, that she knew she couldn't ignore him any longer. Maybe she could just sleep with him a few times and get him out of her system.

Like that will work, the sarcastic voice in her head grumbled.

She moved to sit next to him, handing him one of the water bottles. He placed his on the coffee table, then reached for hers and set it down as well. He shifted to face her and lifted one large hand to cup the side of her cheek. She leaned into his touch.

"Did I tell you how sexy you look tonight?" he asked her, his voice husky.

She nodded. "You look pretty good yourself," she replied, her eyes moving over him in his suit. "You clean up well."

"I was thinking while you were out with Vinnie, and here's what's going to happen Daisy. I'm going to kiss you all over," he said darkly. "And then I'm going to eat you out until you are screaming my name."

Her breath hitched and a rush of moisture hit her already soaked panties. Her eyes were as wide as a cartoon character.

"After I give you at least two orgasms, I plan to sink my cock into your sweet heat and make you come a third time. And I want you to be wearing those boots when I do it."

"That's a pretty ambitious plan," she responded shakily.

He slipped his hand to the back of her neck. "If you don't want that too, you'd better tell me now so I can go."

"OK," she whispered. She realized she was trembling.

"I need to hear you say it Daisy," he said urgently. "Tell me what you want."

She met his gaze confidently. "I want you to fuck me Red," she said boldly, surprised at the vehemence in her tone. "Now."

Red

His heart stopped, the re-started with a thud. Red jumped up and grabbed Daisy's hand. "Where's the bedroom?" he rasped.

The moved up the stairs together without a word, Vinnie trailing behind them.

"He's not going to join us, is he?" Red asked.

Daisy laughed, and the sound filled him with happiness. She gave him a little shove into her bedroom, then moved to close the door behind them as Red flipped the light switch. "Stay Vinnie," she said firmly, pointing at the hallway. The big dog dropped his butt to the floor with a long-suffering sigh as Daisy shut him out.

Red took a quick look around her bedroom. It was comfortable. Not too frilly, but with definite feminine touches. A king-sized bed was against one wall, neatly made, and he headed right over there, unbuttoning his shirt and throwing it over a chair as he walked.

Daisy turned on a lamp in the corner of the room, then moved to turn the overhead light back off. The room dimmed considerably but the corner light and the moon through the window gave it a romantic glow. She moved towards him almost shyly, her gaze on his.

He met her halfway, pulling her into his embrace. He leaned down and kissed her softly. She sighed happily against his lips and moved closer. He grasped the firm curves of her ass, pulling her firmly against his erection. His tongue pushed into her mouth as she began rocking her pelvis against his.

He could feel her small hands running up and down the bare skin of his back. She pulled away and looked at his naked torso curiously. "For some reason I thought you would have more tattoos," she said.

"I have the arm sleeves," he said. "That feels like enough to me."

She nodded, her brow crinkling in confusion.

He leaned down and kissed the tip of her nose. "We have a big problem Daisy," he said.

"What?"

"You're wearing way too many clothes."

He moved around her, intending to unzip her dress, but she stopped him.

"I don't want to talk about my tattoos, or anything about my past tonight," she told him firmly. "Promise me."

He held up his hand. "Scouts honor."

"Were you really a scout?" she asked curiously.

"Of course," he lied. "Now get that damned dress off."

She reached behind herself and pulled the zipper down, the shifted so the dress fell down to her feet, then unclasped her bra, dropping it to the floor as well. She stared at the floor while his gaze ran over her body, clad only in her green silk panties and those knee-high boots.

Her breasts were fuller than he remembered, her dusky rose nipples poking out towards him. Her hips were slim, her belly softly rounded. She was stunning. She reached down and unzipped her boots, kicking them off.

She had faded tattoos running down her arms and legs, above both breasts, and peeking out above her panties on both hips. He moved behind her and saw a tramp stamp emblazoned on her lower back. The tattoos were scattered haphazardly and were mostly amateurish, as if she had been used as practice for beginners. He felt anger rise as he recalled her saying that she had gotten all the tats before she was 16.

Motorcycle club emblems were inked alongside skulls and angry roses. He had no idea what had happened to her but given the MC insignias and the fact that she had been attacked by a club lieutenant, he knew it couldn't have been good.

He moved back to face her. She was still frozen in place, staring at the floor. He wondered how many guys had made her feel bad about the tattoos. Red placed a finger underneath her chin and gently pushed her head up until she met his gaze.

"You are beautiful, standing here in the moonlight," he said firmly. "But you're going to look even more beautiful underneath me."

She shot him a grateful look and moved towards the bed. He followed her, pulling his wallet out and removing a condom before she shucked off his pants and briefs. His cock bounced against his stomach and Daisy's eyes widened.

"Lay down," he instructed. She complied without a word and he shifted onto the bed, settling just off to her side. He leaned down and kissed her lazily while he moved his fingers around one nipple. He circled gently, then increased the pressure. Daisy moaned softly against his mouth.

"You like it when I play with your nipples baby?" he asked softly.

She nodded and her caught the nipple between two fingers, pinching it while pulling out a little bit. Daisy shifted restlessly. He lowered his mouth and circled her with his tongue, while his hand moved over to give her other breast some attention. He could feel her breath quicken.

He trailed kisses across her chest, moving down across her stomach and along her sides. He shifted and kissed his way down one leg. He reached up and pulled her panties down, throwing them over his head, then kissed his way up her other leg. When he got to her glistening sex he pushed her legs apart gently and settled between them, staring at her neatly groomed pussy.

"You have such a pretty pussy," he said, leaning down to spread her folds.

"I had no idea you had such a dirty mouth," she said with a smile.

"That's not the only thing I can do with my mouth," he shot back as he dropped his head and licked her slit from one end to the other.

"Ahh," she garbled, as he continued to lick up and down, up and down. He slowed his movements, circling her opening with his tongue before plunging in to fuck her with his tongue.

Daisy gripped the bedspread in each hand, squeezing her eyes shut. He reached around and found her clit, circling it with his thumb as he continued to lick into her opening. She started thrashing under his mouth and he moved his elbows to hold her thighs in place.

"Red," she panted. "Oh my god."

"I know you're getting close baby," he growled. "Come for me."

As if her body was trained to come at his command she stiffened beneath him then broke apart, wailing as her body spasmed. He lapped up her cream and reduced the pressure on her clit as she came down.

She was silent for a full minute before opening her eyes and looking down at him, a satisfied smile on her face. He slid up her body, resting on top of her, and kissed her until they were both breathless.

"Where did you put that condom?" she asked, reaching down to palm his cock. It jumped happily in her hand.

"Not yet Daisy," he chastised, pulling away from her fingers with reluctance. "I believe I promised you two orgasms first."

She shook her head. "Oh no, that's OK, I can't, I mean, not twice in a row, that never happens."

Fortunately for her, Red loved a challenge. "We'll see about that."

He grabbed a pillow and moved to kneel at the foot of the bed, pulling her ankles to slide her down the mattress towards him. Red pulled until she was at the edge of the mattress, then pulled Daisy's legs over his shoulders, shoving a pillow under her pelvis to angle her up towards him. He lowered his head and began to eat her out as if his life depended on it.

He slipped one long finger inside her, noting that she was still dripping wet. He added a second finger and began pumping in and out roughly while his tongue circled close to her clit.

"Red please," she gasped.

He ignored her and continued circling her around her clit without actually touching it. She was making the most adorable little whining noises as she shoved her pelvis towards his face, trying to direct his tongue to where she needed it. He lifted his head and looked at her flushed face. "Be patient, Daisy," he said.

He moved one finger through her slit, picking up moisture, then slid moved it down along her ass crack. "What are you doing?" she asked.

He circled his finger along her puckered opening. "Just what you think I'm doing," he responded as he gently pressed his finger inside her. When she clenched her internal muscles, he nipped her stomach with his teeth. She gasped and relaxed, and his finger popped inside.

He began to move his slowly inside her while he continued to move the fingers of his other hands inside her channel.

"Oh my god, I never, oh my god," she babbled. He could feel her trembling around his fingers and knew she was close. Without a word he moved his head and took her clit into his mouth, sucking it firmly and sending her crashing over the edge. She came with a long wail, thrashing against the onslaught of his fingers in both of her openings and his tongue on her sensitive bundle of nerves.

She shuddered as she came down, and he gently extricated his fingers, giving her a triumphant look. "What was that about never coming twice?" he asked proudly.

Daisy

Holy. Shit.

Daisy felt shellshocked. Her entire body was vibrating as she came down from her second orgasm. She had never in her life came twice in a row, not even with her vibrator. Red had some talented fingers, and he was pretty good with his tongue too.

She blushed as she remembered him breaching her ass. She had never done that either. She was a 40-year-old anal virgin, she thought to herself with a laugh.

Red stood up from his perch on the floor, his eyes darkening as they slid up her body. He reached down and grasped his cock, giving himself a couple of firm pumps. "You ready for orgasm three?" he asked.

She laughed as she slid back up the bed. "I can't believe you got two of me," she said. "You're magic."

She heard the crinkling of a wrapper and looked over to watch him roll on the condom. Daisy always insisted on condoms to prevent STDs, but she didn't need to worry about getting pregnant. Repeated sexual penetration at a young age had caused endometriosis and scarring in her reproductive system, leading to infertility. The doctors had discovered this soon after she had been rescued from the MC. She felt a stab of anger as she always did when she thought about her choice to have children being stolen from her at such a young age.

Red turned back towards her, his thick cock jutting towards her, and she brought her focus back to the present. Wow. Red was quite a specimen – long and thick. She licked her lips and heard him growl.

"What's your preference?" he asked as he sat on the bed.

She was touched by his courtesy. Smiling, she sat up and answered, "On your back, I want to ride you."

"Good choice," he said approvingly as he reclined on the bed, folding his arms under his head.

Daisy threw one leg over him and moved to straddle his hips. Their eyes met for a long moment and then, still holding his gaze, she began to lower herself slowly onto his cock. He groaned.

She was so wet from those two orgasms that he slid in easily, despite his girth. She bottomed out, her pelvis resting on his, then paused to allow herself to adjust. She felt her muscles relax and began to shift up and down, watching his reaction carefully.

His hips began to pump up to meet hers as she quickened the pace. Red slid his hands out from behind his head and reached up to pinch her nipples, one in each hand. She felt the zing travel down to her core.

Red dragged his hands slowly down her body until he grasped her hips, helping to set a rhythm. She began circling her own tender nipples with her fingers as Red increased their pace even more.

"You look hot as fuck," he growled. "Now work your clit."

She dragged her fingers down to circle her distended bundle of nerves. Like her nipples, her clit was sensitive from their earlier activities. She moaned as she gently massaged herself.

Suddenly she felt her inner muscles tighten. "Oh my god Red," she gasped. "I think I'm going to come again."

"I feel you baby," he said, pounding their hips against each other. As her third orgasm hit her she was dimly aware of Red stiffening underneath her, then shouting her name as he joined her, shooting his warm seed into the condom.

She collapsed against his chest and they both lay there, not moving. The room was quiet other than the sounds of their harsh breaths as they tried to suck in oxygen. Suddenly a high-pitched whine broke the silence.

"What the hell was that?" Red asked.

"Vinnie wants to come in now that we're done," Daisy said as she rolled off him and handed him the Kleenex box. "Do you mind if he comes in, or did you want to do it again?"

Red chuckled. "I'm 42 years old sweetheart," he said as he removed the condom and wrapped it in a tissue. "I'm going to need more than two minutes to recover."

Red

Daisy opened the bedroom door and Vinnie rushed in, looking around the room suspiciously. The giant dog moved in front of Daisy, who was standing gloriously naked near the foot of the bed. She leaned down, sticking her ass in Red's direction, and he felt his cock stir back to life.

"Oh, did you feel left out baby?" she crooned, rubbing the dog between his ears. His tail thumped loudly against the floor. "I know, you were lonely out there, weren't you?"

Vinnie looked up at her with pure adoration and Red felt a little jealous of Vinnie stealing her attention. He shook his head, it wasn't like him to be so clingy.

Daisy padded back towards the bed and Vinnie flopped down to lay on the floor between the bed and the door. He looked relaxed, yet Red could sense the dog's protective vigilance.

"Well, that was fun," Daisy said, shooting a glance at Red. He realized that she had grabbed a robe and was pulling it on, covering herself. His brain cried out in protest as her sexy curves disappeared beneath the fabric. Daisy looked at him expectantly and he realized that she was waiting for him to get up and leave.

"Are you kicking me out?" he asked incredulously.

She looked confused. "I thought we were done. You weren't planning to sleep over, were you?"

Red tried not to feel hurt. "I can go if you want me to," he said slowly, sitting up. "But I'm hoping you don't want me to. I'd love to wake up with you."

"I don't usually do sleepovers," she prevaricated.

"You don't usually have more than one orgasm either," he reminded her smugly. "And yet I gave you three." He patted the bed next to him. "Think what I could do with more practice."

She stood there looking indecisive for what felt like an hour. Red had never wanted a woman to ask him to sleep over this much in his entire life.

"Um, OK, I guess you can stay," she said grudgingly.

He smiled, feeling triumphant. "Well with that effusive invitation, how can I resist? Now get over here and cuddle with me woman."

"I don't—,".

"Yeah yeah, you don't cuddle," he interrupted. "I bet I can change your mind about that too."

And he did.

A few hours later Red awoke with a start. He was trained from all of his years in the military to awaken easily. He looked around, trying to get his bearings in the dark room. What had he heard?

He saw eyes glowing in the darkness and realized that Vinny was standing next to the bed, his head on Daisy's thigh. The dog watched her carefully. Red sat up as Daisy began to thrash around violently.

"No, please no," she sobbed. "Leave me alone! Don't hurt him."

She was having a nightmare. Clearly her dog had realized it before he did. "I. can't. breathe," she gasped haltingly.

Red felt a sharp pinch in his chest. She sounded so scared, so small. He was wondering if he should wake her up when Vinnie started whining loudly, rubbing his giant head back and forth on her thigh as he continued to watch her. Suddenly Daisy sat straight up with a shrill scream.

She looked around, wild eyed. "What? What happened?" she gasped, breathing like she had just ran a marathon at top pace. Vinnie whined again and she reached over to stroke his head. "Oh sweetie, did you wake up again to stop the nightmares? You're such a good boy."

The dog pressed into her shaking hand as she petted him.

"Does this happen a lot?" Red asked quietly. He remembered his first two years out of the service, when his own nightmares came frequently.

She gasped, her head swinging towards him in surprise. "Oh. Shit. I forgot you were here, Red. I'm sorry I woke you up."

He moved closer and rubbed her bare shoulder. She was trembling and her skin felt clammy. "Don't worry about me," he said. "Are you OK?"

"I will be," she said, still stroking Vinnie's head and making kissing faces at him.

She slid out of bed and used the restroom, then returned, still looking shaky. He held his arm out and she went to him without hesitation, draping herself across his chest as he wrapped his arm around her trembling body.

Red felt the mattress dip as Vinnie jumped up, circled around twice then lay down at the foot of the bed by their feet, still watching Daisy. He felt a surge of gratitude that the dog looked after her so well.

Daisy sighed as she snuggled closer, her hand splayed out over his bare abdomen. "Do you want to talk about it?" he asked.

"No. But thanks," she said. He knew better than to push.

She drifted off to sleep a few minutes later, but Red lay awake for a long time, keeping vigil over her with Vinnie. No more nightmares came, and he finally slid into a deep sleep.

The next time Red woke up it was daytime. The sun was out and streaming through the windows. He rolled over, expecting to see Daisy, then made an unmanly squeaking noise as he saw Vinnie laying in the bed next to him. The giant dog's head was on the pillow, and the blanket was pulled up over him as if Daisy had tucked him in before she left. What the hell?

Vinnie opened one eye and stared at Red. He tentatively reached out and stroked the dog's head, and Vinnie sighed, relaxing.

"Thanks for keeping an eye on our girl Vinnie," Red whispered. "You're a good boy."

Vinnie sighed happily and went back to sleep.

Red walked around the room, retrieving his various pieces of clothing, then headed downstairs. Daisy was in the kitchen, eating at the island and reading a book.

"Toaster waffle?" she asked, lifting her plate towards him and wiggling it enticingly. "I have more in the freezer."

"No thanks," he said regretfully. "I have to get to the shop, I have an appointment in an hour."

She nodded and slid off her stool. "OK. I'll walk you to the door."

With a brief detour into the living room to find his suit jacket, they reached the door. Daisy seemed distant again, and he wondered if it was from what they had shared the night before, or because she was upset that he had witnessed her nightmare. Red stopped her as her hand reached for the door handle, and turned her to face him, her back against the door.

He waited until she met his eyes. "Last night was fucking incredible Daisy," he said earnestly. "I've never felt that way before with anyone. I want to keep seeing you. Please don't shut me out."

Her eyes widened in surprise and he knew his instincts had been right.

"I'm not going to judge you Daisy, and I'm not going to hurt you either," he continued. "I know you're scared, and I am too, but I just want to be with you and see where this thing goes."

Hopefully it went the way Mitch and Penny's relationship had gone. When he had watched them get married yesterday Red has been surprised to feel a strong desire that it had been him and Daisy up there instead. The realization had rocked him to the core.

"Besides, I woke up in bed snuggling with your weirdo dog," he said, lightening the mood. "If that doesn't show how much I like you, I don't know what does."

Daisy was silent for a long moment, then she nodded. She grasped his face in her hands and lifted up on her toes to kiss him lightly on the lips. "You want to come over tonight?" she asked. "I can make you dinner."

He smiled brightly as he felt his soul lighten. "Try and stop me."

Daisy

Daisy whistled to herself as she put on Vinnie's leash. It was a beautiful summer day and she was feeling quite cheerful. It probably had something to do with her waking up to find Red's head between her legs. She loved starting the day off with orgasms. How had she lived so many years without it?

As she walked along with Vinnie she thought about how much things had changed in the last three months. Since that first night together after the wedding, Red had slept over at her house more than he had slept at his own place.

They had fallen into a comfortable rhythm together, walking Vinnie, cooking dinner, going for hikes, reading or watching movies together. Daisy had never imagined that she could have a relationship like this. Red was caring and solicitous but also didn't interfere with her being her own woman and having her own life. There were things that annoyed them about each other but neither of them tried to change the other. Their relationship felt like a true partnership.

Well, a partnership with sex. Lots and lots of sex. She had never thought she had a particularly high sex drive until Red came along. They both had the stamina of twenty-year-olds. She smiled to herself. Maybe they should talk about moving in together soon? He was at her place most nights anyway.

Daisy heard a car screech around the corner, and she pulled Vinnie up beside her to protect him.

Stupid tourists, she thought, *always driving like maniacs.*

The car stopped and a man jumped out, leaving the driver's side door open. "Well, well, well, if it isn't our little Daisy."

She looked up at the man for the first time and her heart stopped. It was one her father's so-called lieutenants. She didn't know his real name, everyone in the club had called him Whiskey. He was 23 years older than the last time she had seen him, but she still recognized him as one of the men who had sexually assaulted her as a teen. Every muscle in her body froze in shock.

When she didn't respond he continued, "What's the matter Daisy, you too stuck up to say hello to one of your old boyfriends?"

Her stomach roiled and she willed herself not to throw up. Vinnie growled next to her, his whole body coiled with tension.

"What do you want?" she finally asked, pleased with how strong her voice sounded. "We have no business together."

Whiskey walked a little closer and she noticed the bulge in his waistband when he ran his finger over the butt of the gun he had stashed there. "We have a lot of business sweetheart," he said, his voice dark and vibrating with anger. "Like why I've been in the pen for 23 years because of you. That's a long time for me not to have some fun. I was thinking we could get back together, for old time's sake. You always were good for a little fun."

Daisy knew in that moment that if he got a hold of her he would torture and kill her. She knew how these people thought. She remembered the last guy who had come for her.

"Fire!" she yelled, as loud as she could. She remembered reading that people ignored cries for help but were conditioned to come assist if there was a fire. "Fire! Fire!"

"What the fuck are you screeching about bitch? Come with me and I won't kill your mutt too. Although I should after he bit Tango."

Whiskey removed the gun from his waistband and advanced towards Daisy. She was rooted to the spot but yelled "Fire!" again as loud as she could.

The next few seconds happened in a blur. She felt Whiskey try to grab her wrist. She pulled back, trying to escape his hold. Vinnie lunged forward, growling ominously. She heard a shot, quickly followed by a sharp fiery pain in her stomach. She fell back, slamming her head on the concrete sidewalk with a dull. She heard Whiskey scream, "Get off me". And the world went dark.

Red

Red heard his cell phone ring. "Hey Mitch, how…".

His friend interrupted his greeting. "It's Daisy, she's been hurt."

Red froze, fear coursing through his body. "What happened?"

"I'm pulling up outside the shop now, let's go."

Red raced outside and jumped into the passenger seat of Mitch's squad car. Mitch hit the lights and took off quickly. He briefed Red as they went.

"She's been shot," he started. "We're not sure how bad it is yet."

Red felt all the breath whoosh out of his body. "What do you know?"

"According to witnesses the perp jumped out the car and cornered her. He pulled a gun. Daisy yelled for help and the guy grabbed her. Vinnie went for him, but he got a couple of shots off on the way down."

"Did you catch the asshole?" Red asked.

"Vinnie did. Held the guy by his throat until we got there. Guy was so scared he pissed his pants." Mitch smiled grimly. "We sent him to the hospital to treat his bites."

Red looked around. "This isn't the way to the hospital, where's Daisy?"

"Still on scene. Vinnie won't let EMS get near her," Mitch responded. "We've called Animal Services."

Mitch screeched to a stop behind an ambulance and Red was out the door before the car came to a complete stop. He raced over, his heart in his chest. Daisy lay unconscious on the sidewalk in a pool of blood. Vinnie stood over at her, keeping an eye on the bystanders.

"Vinnie!" Red called, keeping his voice low and calm. The dog wagged his tail at him, then nudged Daisy with his nose, whining.

"I know buddy, I can see her," he said calmly. He dropped to his knees next to Daisy and pet the dog's head while his eyes scanned her body. She was breathing, but blood was seeping out of a wound in her abdomen. She was still, so still.

The EMS guys approached, and Vinnie growled at them menacingly, moving to stand protectively over Daisy's body. Red looked at the closest guy. "Kneel down where you are," he told the guy.

"What?"

"Kneel on the sidewalk, trust me."

The paramedic knelt a few feet away and Red moved to his feet. Red stood up and walked over to the guy, then started patting his head. "Friend Vinnie," Red said soothingly, gesturing to the paramedic. "Friend. He's gonna help your momma."

Vinnie sit down next to Daisy, at ease. The paramedic looked at Red incredulously, then walked on his knees towards Daisy. Vinnie watched him but did not interfere.

"We need to get her on a backboard," the paramedic said. "Can you get that mutt out of here?"

Red grabbed Vinnie's leash and coaxed the dog over to the grass, sitting next to him. "We'll sit right here and watch your momma, OK Vinnie?"

They watched the paramedics put compression on the wound, calling out vitals. "I've got a pulse, but it's low and thready," one called. "Let's get her to the hospital."

They lifted her onto the gurney and rolled her towards the ambulance. Vinnie growled and tried to follow.

"Let's say goodbye," Red said with a comforting rub on the head. He and Vinnie approached, and the dog went on his hind legs, licking Daisy's face. She didn't move.

"I'm going to get Vinnie home Daisy," he told her, even though he wasn't sure if Daisy could hear him. "I'll be there soon. Hang in there baby, we love you." He leaned down and kissed her forehead, cursing himself that he had never said those words to her while she was conscious. He had been afraid to freak her out, and now it might be too late.

Mitch came to stand next to him, placing a warm hand on his shoulder. "Let's get Vinnie home then I'll take you to the hospital."

Three hours later Red was pacing the waiting room of the hospital while Mitch watched. After getting Vinnie settled back at Daisy's house they had come straight to the hospital to find that Daisy was in surgery.

"Who's here for Daisy Hunnicutt?" Red's pacing was interrupted by the doctor.

"I am," Red called, striding over to him. "How is she?"

"Are you family?" the doctor asked.

"I'm her boyfriend, Red O'Brian."

The doctor said, "I can only confirm that she's doing ok then," he said, looking down at his file. "You're not listed as her emergency contact."

"We're the emergency contact," someone said behind him.

Red turned to see an older couple rushing into the room. Red immediately pegged the man as former military, he could see it in his stance. "Samuel and Suzanne Johnston, here for Daisy Hunnicutt," the man said to the doctor. "How is she?"

"She's recovering from a gunshot wound to the abdomen," the doctor said. "Fortunately, the bullet didn't damage any major organs, but she did lose a lot of blood. We operated and repaired the damage."

"Can we talk to her?" Suzanne asked. "Is she awake?"

The doctor shook his head. "It looks like she hit her head good when she fell," he answered. "There's some swelling around the brain and we will probably keep her unconscious until the swelling goes down. But you can see her in a few minutes after she gets back to a room. I'll have the nurse come get you."

The doctor nodded at the group and left.

Suzanne turned to Red and Mitch. "Did I hear someone say boyfriend?" she asked curiously.

Red stuck his hand out. "I'm Red O'Brian. Daisy and I have been dating for a few months."

Samuel shook his hand with a firm grip and an appraising look. "Nice to meet you Red. So you're the guy who's been spending so much time with our Daisy?"

"Yes. Who are you exactly?"

Red learned that Suzanne and Samuel were Daisy's foster parents. He recalled her mentioning in passing once that she had been in a foster home, but he hadn't pried for the details. He had no idea she was still in contact with them, but they had clearly heard about him.

The Johnstons were obviously protective of Daisy. It had been a long time since Red had been interrogated by someone's parents, but they had a long wait before they could see Daisy during which Suzanne and Samuel dragged his life story out of him, as well as details about their relationship.

Mitch laughed. "You two are good interrogators, let me guess, police?"

Samuel told him he had been a cop in Seattle for thirty years, and Suzanne had managed a women's crisis line.

At long last a nurse came to let them know that Daisy was set up in a room. Mitch left to work on his reports while Red and the Johnstons headed to the room. Red's breath hitched as he saw Daisy laying in the bed, hooked up to machines and looking so pale.

He moved to her side and took her hand, feeling more helpless than he ever had in his life. He didn't leave her side for two days.

Daisy

Daisy fought her way through the fog. She heard beeping and opened one eye. It looked like a hospital. What was she doing there? She opened the other eye. Jesus, it felt like someone had hit her in the head with a brick. Wait, had someone hit her in the head with a brick?

She turned her head gingerly. Red was slumped in a chair, sleeping. "Red?" she croaked.

It hadn't been more than a whisper but Red immediately sat up, wide awake. He grabbed her hand. "Daisy? Oh my god, you're finally awake. Thank god."

He rubbed his thumb on her wrist. "How do you feel baby?"

She shook her head and winced. "Terrible. What happened? Did someone hit me in the head?"

He watched her carefully. "No, you hit your head on the sidewalk when you fell."

"How did I....? Oh my god, that asshole shot me," she gasped as the memories returned. "Where's Vinnie? Is he OK?"

She heard the beeping speed up as the panic hit her.

"Shh, it's ok Daisy," he soothed, rubbing his other hand across her jaw. "Vinnie's fine. He wasn't hurt at all. He's been staying with Mitch and Penny."

"What happened after I was shot?" she asked. "I think I passed out."

Red nodded. "Vinnie took the guy down," he explained, clear admiration in his voice. "Held him down by the throat until the police came. He's gone back to prison. Vinnie saved your life – again."

"That's my boy," she said weakly. Then everything was quiet again.

The next time Daisy woke up she realized her foster parents were in the room. "Daisy, sweetheart, you gave us a scare," Suzanne told her, leaning down to give her a kiss on the forehead. "Sorry we weren't here when you woke up the first time, we had just popped down to get lunch when you woke up."

Samuel reached down and rubbed her shoulder. "You know kid, if you wanted us to visit you, all you had to do was ask," he said gruffly.

"Thanks for driving down," Daisy said.

"Oh no, we didn't drive down," Suzanne said. "Sam called in some favors and got us a helicopter ride. It would have been exciting if not for the circumstances."

"Where's Red?" Daisy asked, looking around. "He was here when I got up the first time."

Suzanne smiled. "He just went to the rest room. That boy has been by your side for two days. Refused to even go home and sleep. He seems quite taken with you."

Daisy felt a rush of warmth, followed by a cold, dark fear. What if Red had gotten hurt because of her?

The thought made her nauseous. She loved him, she realized with a start. It would kill her if something happened to him because of her terrible past. This latest incident had shown her that the MC would never leave her alone. She needed to protect him.

She fell back asleep.

"You should go home," Daisy told Red the next day. She had managed to stay awake most of the day, and the doctors had deemed her to be recovering nicely. "They'll be releasing me tomorrow and you need to open your shop."

Red's brow furrowed in confusion. "The shop can wait, Daisy."

She shook her head and straightened her spine. She had to be strong. She had to keep him safe.

"I appreciate you being here Red, but we've been spending a lot of time together these last few months. I realized that I need some space."

Her voice trembled as she continued, "I think we should spend some time apart. My foster parents are going to stay with me for a while to help out."

Red moved to sit on the side of the bed, taking both of her hands. "Daisy, what's going on? Talk to me baby."

She shook her head. "Nothing's going on. I just need to focus on recovering and you have a business to run."

Red stared at her for a long moment, clearly not believing her. The silence stretched as he watched her.

"Daisy," he finally said, his words careful. "Why are you pushing me away? Is it because of the, um, incident?"

Daisy felt a surge of anger. "The incident?" she said, her voice raising in pitch. "You mean the way someone tried to kill me the other day? Don't you get it Red, they'll just keep coming for me. It's not safe. It's not safe for me, and it's not safe for you or Vinnie. I don't even know if I should stay here in Diamond Bay or move someplace else."

Red stiffened. "What's this really about Daisy?" he asked. "Who's after you? Who was that guy who attacked you?"

She had never told him the story before, although she had a feeling he had put bits and pieces together. "Look Red, you're a great guy, but you need someone who isn't damaged."

"You're not damaged, Daisy. How can you even say that?"

"I am," she insisted. "That guy who came to kill me? He was in my father's motorcycle gang. He was one of the guys who passed me around when I was a teenager, who shared me, who used my body and marked my skin to show the world I belonged to them."

Red's eyes widened and she plowed ahead.

"I helped take them down, I gave evidence against them," her voice wobbled, and she cleared her throat. "I betrayed them, and they all went to jail. I'll never be safe. And you'll never be safe if you're with me. I can't let anything happen to you."

"Daisy..."

"No. Please, go Red. This thing between us, it ends now. I need to be alone and figure out where I go next."

Red looked like she had just stabbed him in the heart, and she understood how he felt – she felt the same. He stood up.

"We're not done Daisy," he vowed. "You've been through a lot and I'll give you some space, but I'm not giving up on you. Whatever happens, we'll figure it out together. I love you Daisy. More than anything."

A sob escaped her throat as she shook her head. "And that's why you'll never be safe. Goodbye Red."

As she watched Red leave the room, the tears finally began to fall.

Two weeks later...

"When are you going to call him, Daisy?"

Suzanne was standing in the doorway watching her carefully.

"What do you mean?" Daisy asked.

Suzanne gave her a no-nonsense glare and moved to sit on the coffee table by Daisy's knees. "You've been sitting on this couch moping for two weeks, I think this has gone on long enough."

"Moping?" Daisy said incredulously. "I've been recovering from a freaking gunshot wound."

Suzanne stared her down. "You and I both know you're not feeling bad from the wound, which I remind you didn't hit any organs." Her foster mother had never been one to coddle people.

Her voice softened. "You forget how well I know you, Daisy. You're moping because you miss Red. And judging by all the times he has texted, called or sent you presents, he misses you too."

Daisy shook her head. "It's over. It was never going to work out between us."

"That's funny, I could have sworn you were in love with him. He was the first person you asked for when you woke up after surgery."

Suzanne grabbed her hand. "I know the shooting shook you up, sweetie, but the guy didn't budge from your side for two full days. He just sat there watching you sleep. It's obvious he loves you too. Sam and I talked to him quite a bit, he seems like a good guy for you."

"I can't risk it Suzanne, I can't risk him being hurt, you know how these people are."

"Are you sure that you're worried about him being hurt Daisy?" Suzanne asked, her eyebrow rising nearly to her hairline. "Because from where I'm sitting it seems more like you're worried about YOU getting hurt. And I don't mean from the motorcycle gang."

Daisy shook her head, and to her horror she felt her eyes filling with tears. She had cried more in the last two weeks than she had in her whole life. The shooting had ruined her sense of stability and pushing Red away had made her feel emptier than she ever had in her life.

"I never thought you'd turn into a coward."

"I'm not a coward!" Daisy denied hotly.

"You're letting them have power over you Daisy." Suzanne's voice softened. "You refusing to live your life, rejecting a wonderful man who loves you, living in fear...you're letting them win. You're letting the people who tried to break you win. Don't do it. You're stronger than that. I know you are."

Daisy stared at her for a long time, the words sinking in. "I miss him. And Vinnie misses him too."

"Ah, now you get it," Suzanne said, "I see the lightbulb going on in your brain. Just promise me one thing."

"What?" Daisy asked.

"Take a shower before you go get your man. You're starting to stink."

Red

"We're closed."

Red heard the bell on the shop door ring and started heading towards the front. "I can make an appointment with you for tomorrow."

He rounded the corner and dropped the bottle of ink in his hand. "Daisy."

She was in the lobby, looking curiously at the art on the wall. In all the time they had been together, Daisy had never stepped foot in his shop before. She had always refused to come in.

She looked at him with a tremulous smile. "This place isn't what I imagined," she said. "It's so clean and bright." She pointed at the displays on the wall. "I love your art."

"What are you doing here Daisy?" he asked, walking slowly towards her. It had been two weeks since he had heard from her, and he had just about given up hope. "You haven't responded to any of my messages."

"I know. I'm sorry Red, I just needed some time to think."

He nodded. "Are you done thinking?"

Her eyes searched his face. He forced himself to remain still.

"I've never had a long-term relationship before," she began.

"Yeah, I've clued into that," he shot back.

She sucked her lips in. "I deserve that, I guess."

"You really hurt me Daisy," he responded. "When I saw you laying on that sidewalk in a puddle of blood, I thought I had lost you." He got a little choked up and cleared his throat. "Then I lost you anyway."

"I want a tattoo."

He reeled back in shock. "What?"

"These marks on my body, the ones I hide, they were put on me when I was too young and scared to consent," she said. "Now I want something that is mine. I want you to put something beautiful on me Red, to remind me that I'm a survivor."

She stepped closer and took his hand, wrapping her small fingers around his. "The day I got shot, I started the morning happier than I had ever been. Because of you. I was thinking about how we should move in together, how I wanted to wake up with you every morning."

He gave her a small smile of encouragement and she continued. "And then I woke up in the hospital and my first thought was that I could have died without telling you that I love you."

His heart leaped with joy, but he stayed silent, knowing there was more.

"Then I thought, it would kill me if something happened to you because of me. If someone hurt you because of me," she continued. "That would be worse than anything they could do to me. If they knew about you, they would hurt you to get to me."

"No one's going to hurt me Daisy," he told her. "You can't live your life in fear."

"There's more," she said. "The thing that freaked me out even more was realizing that the only thing that would be worse than someone taking you away from me would be if you left me on your own." Her eyes filled with tears and his heart melted a little bit more.

"Daisy, we both know there are no guarantees." He stepped closer to her, so she had to look up at him. "But we love each other, and that's all that matters. Everything else is noise."

"I'm sorry Red," she whispered. "I want to try to make this work. Can you forgive me for pushing you away again? I can't promise I won't hurt you again, but I can promise to try."

He leaned down until his lips were a breath away from hers. "Tell me again about how you love me."

"I love you Red. Truly."

He claimed her mouth in a long, passionate kiss. "Well, then let's get you a tattoo."

Epilogue - Red

Two years later...

"Red, you'll never guess what the baby did!"

Red came out of the kitchen to see Daisy standing in the hallway with a big smile. As always, Vinnie was right by her side. On her other side, their new family member quivered with excitement.

Red picked up the chunky little Great Dane puppy. They had seen him at an adoption fair and adopted him on the spot. Vinnie was slowing down as he aged, and at first he had been hesitant about having a little brother, but he had quickly adapted to the hyper puppy who followed him everywhere and tried to emulate his every move.

He and Daisy hadn't decided on a name for the puppy yet, so they'd taken to calling him "the baby".

"What did you do little guy?" Red asked, as the puppy licked his face.

"He saw Vinnie lifting his leg to pee and for the first time, he lifted his leg too," Daisy said proudly. "He peed like a big boy."

Red set the puppy down and leaned in to press a quick kiss on Daisy's lips. "I married a weirdo," he told her affectionately. "I can't believe you're excited about the dog peeing."

"Oh yeah, I'm the weirdo," she said. "Who's the one cooking homemade food for these guys now?" she asked.

"It's healthier," he protested. He patted Vinnie's head and the dog closed his eyes happily. "Besides, Vinnie is getting older. We need to keep him around."

She shook her head and leaned in for a hug. His arms circled around her and he brought her close. It had been two years since she got shot, and he had moved in right after they got back together.

Six months later he convinced her to marry him, and it had been the happiest day of his life. Mitch had been the best man and Suzanne the maid of honor. Sam had given her away. Vinnie had, of course, been the ring bearer.

They hadn't had any more trouble with Daisy's old family. Mitch had assured him that after what had happened, the parole board would hesitate to let anyone else from the MC out of prison early. So far, so good.

They had built a happy life together here in Diamond Bay. His shop was thriving, and Daisy continued to work as Town Services manager. They had close knit circle of good friends. Plus, they had the dogs, their own little family.

"You know what's even cooler than hearing about the baby's latest accomplishments?" he asked.

"What?"

"Seeing my wife naked."

She laughed and patted his chest. "OK big guy, let's go upstairs."

***

Did you like this story? Show the love and leave me a review. Reviews are like puppies, they make you feel happy.

Be sure to keep reading for a special except from "Until You Came Along", available now with select retailers.

Special Preview

Until You Came Along by Rose Bak

Jen heard the rumbling from all the way in the kitchen. Wiping her hands on a towel, she walked to the front porch to watch the two large buses drive up the long driveway to the farmhouse. Belching smoke, they idled and came to a stop, one behind the other.

Although it wasn't even 10 a.m. yet the sun shone brightly in the summer sky, showcasing the dust left in the wake of the parked buses. A bird squawked loudly in the sudden silence as a serious looking young woman scurried out of the first bus, glasses askew, a clipboard gripped in one hand, cellphone in another. Two large mountains of men followed her, hulking shadows.

"Jen Oliver? The band is here. We'll just come in and...." she moved to enter the house, but Jen stood her ground, blocking the door.

"Where are they?" she asked the woman, her tone icy. "And who are you exactly?"

The woman looked flustered for a brief moment before her stern mask fell back down again. She shuffled her cell phone into the hand with the clipboard and stuck out her now-free hand to shake. "I'm Simone. I manage the band."

Jen ignored her hand. "Well, manage them out of those buses. They don't get to send the help out to greet their sister."

Simone looked confused as she dropped her hand back to her side. "They're all sleeping. They had a late night. We'll just come in and check...."

"Still up all night and sleeping all day, huh? That's been the same since they were teenagers." Jen shook her head. On the farm they had all been taught the value of hard work – up before dawn, work all day, and early to bed. Somehow those lessons hadn't really stuck with her brothers despite her grandparents' best efforts over the years.

Of course, the boys, as she still thought of them, had been away from the farm for ten years now, chasing fame and fortune as the biggest boy band to hit the charts since N Sync. Like the band that came before them, the Oliver Boys had grown up but continued to enchant teenage girls across the world with their pop tunes.

Simone clearly felt protective of the boys. "They played last night in Wichita you know," she said sternly. "The show went until almost midnight, then they met the fans and press for hours after."

"By meet the fans and press do you mean got drunk and partied?" Jen's tone did little to hide her opinion of the boys and their reputation for debauched partying.

Simone shook her head. "They've mostly settled down now. There's not as much partying as there used to be when they were younger. But they still need to make an effort to meet people, it's part of the job. Now we'll just come in and...."

Jen shook her head. "Well," she drawled. "When they wake up from their so-called job, you send them on in. The rest of you need to find some other place to bunk. I'm not running a hotel for drunken roadies here."

A slight movement behind Simone caught Jen's eyes. One of the giant men flanking Simone shook with repressed laughter, his mouth twisted in a smirk but his face otherwise impassive. Jen looked at him for the first time. He was the size of a small tank, several inches over 6 feet tall, with impossibly wide shoulders and large biceps. His hair was a dark blond, "dishwater blonde" her grandma would call it, worn military short. He was dressed all in black, and she noticed a gun on the shoulder holster. Jen wondered why he felt he needed a gun out here in the middle of nowhere. She felt him watching her and she raised her eyes to his, a shiver of awareness coursing through her, although she couldn't make out his eyes behind the dark sunglasses.

"Miss Oliver..." Simone started again.

"Jen"

"OK, then, Jen, we need to do a security sweep before the boys come in. If you could just move aside, we'll get started." Simone nodded decisively.

"A security—-what the hell are you talking about?"

Simone turned to the man who'd been staring at Jen earlier. "This is Nick, he's head of security for the band. He'll be doing a security sweep and assessment with Brian here," she pointed at the second silent man.

"We don't need a security sweep. This place is as safe as it comes. We don't even lock the doors in these parts."

Simone shook her head again, vibrating with irritation and clearly not used to people disobeying her orders. "No way. The boys don't go anywhere without a security check ahead of time. I'm afraid I have to insist."

Jen shot her a look filled with venom, her tone as cold as ice. "You can insist all you like but this is my property. You have no right to it, and neither do the boys. Y'all can just run along now, I'm not having some ginormous strangers poking around my property. Don't make me sic the dogs on you." Simone's mouth dropped open.

This was an empty threat. Jen's three dogs looked mean, but they were incurably friendly. They were just as likely to lick a person to death as bite them. Jen had a sneaking suspicion that if someone tried to kill her the dogs would jump over her body and leave with the killer. But these music people didn't need to know that. If there was one thing Jen hated, it was music people. They were way too self-important and proud.

"Excuse me ma'am," the guy called Nick interrupted.

"Jen," she repeated, a trace of irritation in her tone.

He inclined his head. "Sorry. Jen. As Simone mentioned, I'm head of security for the band. We've had some issues and I would be very appreciative if my team could just poke around for a bit and make sure there's nothing amiss." His tone was deferential and charming, which only heightened Jen's suspicions.

"What kind of issues?"

"I'm afraid I'm not at liberty to discuss that ma—I mean Jen."

"Then I'm afraid I'm not at liberty to grant you access to my property. You step foot off that driveway, and I'll shoot you myself, right after I set the dogs on you. And you," she pointed at Simone, "better make sure no one bothers me again until I see those boys on my porch." She spun on her heel and slammed the door. It was going to be a long day.

For more of Jen's story, check out Until You Came Along by Rose Bak. Available on select retailers.

About the Author

Rose Bak has been obsessed with reading since she got her first library card at age five. A passionate reader and a frequent blogger, she writes both fiction and nonfiction. Rose lives in the Pacific Northwest with her family and special needs dogs.

Please sign up for my newsletter[1] to get a free book and keep up to date on all the Rose Bak romance news.

1.	*https://storyoriginapp.com/giveaways/62ee758e-068f-11eb-904e-c373f6014fe1*

Other Books by Rose Bak

The Diamond Bay Contemporary Romance Series
Brand New Penny
Fresh as a Daisy
Right as Rain
The Good with Numbers Holiday Novella Contemporary Romance Series
Love Unmasked
The Thanksgiving Scrooge
Maid for Christmas
Countdown to Love
Valentine's Lottery
The Oliver Boys Band Contemporary Romance Series
Until You Came Along
Rock Star Teacher
Rock Star Writer
Rock Star Neighbor
The Bite-Sized Shifters Series
Wolf Doctor
Loving the Holidays Series
Dating Santa
The Reunited Series
Together Again
Standalone
Beach Wedding

Non-fiction
What to Do If You Find a Cougar in Your Living Room: Self-Care in an Uncaring World

Catch up with these and other stories. Join my newsletter for more information[1] or follow my author page on your favorite retailer.

9 7 9 8 2 0 1 7 9 1 8 2 7